11/15/93

Chivers

A TIME FOR PIRATES

When Paul Harris, entrepreneur and man about the Far East, rescues Jean Hyde from a rioting mob in Kuala Lumpur, he is unwittingly doing himself a bad turn. This beautiful blonde is the wife of a geologist looking for oil on behalf of a Chinese company, and Paul is totally committed in his fight to save Malaysia from Communism, in whatever guise it appears. So he goes into the oil business himself and the real trouble starts. It is only after two kidnap attempts, a near-fatal fight with a Manchu thug and the firing of his house, that he dares to admit to himself his shattering suspicion: the man who wants him dead is a friend.

A TIME FOR PIRATES

Gavin Black

·BLACK·
DAGGER
·CRIME·

First published 1971
by
William Collins
This edition 1993 by Chivers Press
published by arrangement with
the author

ISBN 0 7451 8619 X

British Library Cataloguing in Publication Data available

Printed and bound in Great Britain by
Redwood Books, Trowbridge, Wiltshire

TO MY SISTER, RITA MacGINITIE

FOREWORD

GAVIN BLACK is the pen-name of Oswald Wynd, whose first
novel *Black Fountains* was published in 1947. He wrote thir-
teen more novels under his own name and in 1960 published
Suddenly at Singapore, the first of fifteen Gavin Black thrillers.
In a career spanning forty years, he produced twenty-nine
fine books, the last in 1989.

Always popular, he became a world bestseller with *The
Ginger Tree*, the haunting story of a Scotswoman who falls in
love with a Japanese diplomat, bears his son – whom she is
not allowed to keep – and picks up the wreckage to make her
own life in Japan. THE GINGER TREE was made into a highly
successful mini-series for television, screened on BBC-2,
throughout the United States and on NHK-TV in Japan.

Oswald Wynd was born in Japan and stayed there until he
was eighteen. Although he now lives, at the age of eighty, in
the fishing village of Crail on the Fife coast, his work is an
ongoing love affair with the Far East, where he spent much of
his life. Most of his books have an Asian setting. Everything
is well observed – the hot, teeming alleys of the cities, the
dark menace of the jungle, the terrifying power of the criminal underworld.

Above all, he captures the values, fears and hopes of men
and women in Asia – particularly at the interface between
European businessmen or officials and native Chinese or
Malays. The false smile, the resentment, the violence always
just below the surface – all reflect the constant enigma of a
raw new society centred on the individual, clashing with an
older, more subtle world where subordination to the group is
all. A Black Dagger revival of his work is particularly timely
when the countries of the East are assuming ever greater
political and economic significance.

Oswald Wynd brings this vivid understanding of the East
to most of his books, of which *A Time For Pirates*, first published in 1971, is a distinguished example. It starts with a mob
rioting in Kuala Lumpur, capital of newly independent and
unstable Malaysia, torn by tensions between Western en-
trepreneurs, communist terrorists still seeking power, an

unpopular but wealthy Chinese community – the Jews of the East – and Malays ranging from the poor to the obscenely rich. Scottish entrepreneur Paul Harris rescues Jean Hyde from the rioters. She is blonde, beautiful and married to a geologist searching for oil on behalf of a Chinese company Min Kow Lin.

From this chance encounter Harris realises he has stumbled into something murky. Why is the exploration concealed as prospecting for less valuable minerals or buying a rubber plantation? How does Mr Akamoro of the Japanese Hawakami Corporation fit in? What is Harris's old friend the playboy Tunku Batim Salong really up to? Is there a communist or capitalist hidden agenda that will deny the poor of Malaysia the benefits that oil might bring?

Assisted by his humourless Sikh book-keeper Bahadur, Harris seeks for the truth, finding obstruction and violence at every corner. Jean Hyde is attractive enough, but he doesn't trust her:

She walked as though conscious of an audience . . . the mood was clearly carefree, perhaps a bit too heavily defined as such, and it made a malt drinker on a hatch cover wonder what he should be bracing himself for.

As they laze in the sun on his yacht, he casually accuses her of being involved in an attempt to kidnap him, an accessory to his potential murder. In the sudden taut atmosphere she clutches for a way out in a dialogue that shows the author's skill at making the commonplace electric with significance:

Our previous contacts hadn't brought us very close. This one was beginning to. I was conscious of those thighs . . . one of her hands came up and travelled over the back of my shirt to the area of the karate chop bruising.

'Take me down to your cabin, Paul.'
'I don't think so.'
'I'm not your line?'
'What are you offering? Reparations?'
'Sort of. Not tempted?'
'I have a sensitive neck.'
She laughed. 'You think you know everything, Paul. But you don't. Not until you've had me . . .'

The plot spirals from minor commercial skulduggery to top level political intrigue. Harris survives two murderous kidnap attempts and narrowly escapes with his life when his house is burnt down at night by the communist Peoples' Liberation Front. In a brilliant denouement he is forced to conclude that the architect of all this mayhem must be a Westerner with secret links to Peking – and that it can only be a man he has always regarded as a friend.

MICHAEL HARTLAND

Michael Hartland spent twenty years in government service, ending as a diplomat working with intelligence and the United Nations. A full-time writer since his first novel *Down Among the Dead Men* was a bestseller in 1983, his series featuring M.I.6 officer Sarah Cable often has Far East backgrounds – most recently *The Year of the Scorpion*, set against the struggle to destroy communism in post Tian'an Men China. Now one of our leading thriller writers, Michael Hartland is translated into fourteen languages and adapted for radio, film and television. He is a literary critic for *The Times*, and *Sunday Times*, and presents radio and television programmes on real-life espionage.

THE BLACK DAGGER CRIME SERIES

The Black Dagger Crime series is a result of a joint effort between Chivers Press and a sub-committee of the Crime Writers' Association, consisting of Marian Babson, Peter Chambers and Peter Lovesey. It is designed to select outstanding examples of every type of detective story, so that enthusiasts will have the opportunity to read once more classics that have been scarce for years, while at the same time introducing them to a new generation who have not previously had the chance to enjoy them.

A TIME FOR PIRATES

CHAPTER I

THE MINI ahead of me was tucked in close to the belching exhaust of a huge, vibrating furniture van, the driver of the little box apparently getting worried about the danger of carbon monoxide poisoning. The Mini yapped away with its horn like a terrier trying to shift a stubborn cow. A long line of cars behind my Mercedes were expressing fury, too, but I kept my hands firmly away from the klaxon ring, remembering that traffic temper is a beaten path towards the coronary.

Some kind of procession along the main shopping street at right angles to us was causing the hold up. The furniture van blocked most of my view but to the right of it I could just see a biggish crowd at the intersection. No one seemed to be carrying banners, which rather ruled out protest, and it could simply be an outsize Chinese funeral. I switched off the radio and wound down my window, listening for cymbals and possibly a brass band. There was no music or professional lamentations, just shouting.

At two-fifteen pm on any day in the year Kuala Lumpur is a very hot city. I shut the window again to preserve the kind of air conditioning with which a Mercedes cossets its owner and sat there telling myself that it really didn't matter if I wasn't in the office until three.

The Mercedes was close in to a line of empty parked cars with a pavement beyond on which there didn't seem to be any shoppers. I looked across the street and couldn't see people walking there either. Then I noticed that a considerable number of stores had wooden shutters up over their frontages and at others clerks were busy fitting these. The shuttered shop is a tropic storm signal.

I tried the radio again, pushing the button for our local station, getting a cookery lesson in Malay that didn't seem likely to be interrupted for a news flash. An empty down lane tempted me to try a U-turn and escape from a tension area but a check showed that I'd pushed too close to the Mini for this manoeuvre without some reversing and there was a Ford on my rear bumper.

About ten yards up the pavement on my left was a store whose owner had shown faith in the stability of our social structure with the kind of display area that couldn't be shuttered in civic disturbances. The shop faced the future in a glitter of glass and chromium. A massive sign over the new frontage said: FONG WANG FOH, ELECTRICAL REQUIREMENTS. I had to offer a quick tribute to good selling. There was nothing diffident about Mr Foh, he wasn't displaying merchandise there was a chance you might fancy, but telling you that you had to have his stuff, illustrating your need under high-powered strip lighting. The lighting had been switched off but the sun had taken over and behind glass was a big area packed with the basics for contemporary living, hi-fi sets, television, and six foot by three deep-freezers.

Mr Foh represented contemporary progressive capitalism sinking roots in the Oriental scene. That's fine, but out here there is a snag. Malaysia has one of the highest per capita income rates in South East Asia but this still hasn't pushed itself up to anything like the purchasing power of one thousand US dollars a year, which leaves a high percentage of the population unable to do anything more than window shop, and quite often with hate in their hearts.

We'd had window shopper trouble before and this pedestrian uprising at a cross roads could be more of the same. I was now conscious of sitting in the kind of car which has become . . . except to owners . . . an unloved Oriental status symbol, closely associated with Chinese towkays who tend to be showy about their wealth. At least fifty per cent of the well-heeled involved in kidnapping incidents have been pulled out of transport like mine.

Suddenly the van moved, jumping forward as though prodded. The Mini didn't follow at once, it could be that fumes had slowed down driver reaction. Horns clamoured from behind. The Mini jerked away but was too late for what had been available space ahead, this taken over at astounding speed by people pouring down from the intersection. The little car stopped and was surrounded.

I had moved forward but braked while there was still twenty feet between me and the crowd. The Ford made use of the space given it to go into the dramatic U-turn I'd been contemplating and the other cars in the row took their cue and did the same, all accelerating away like the start of a rally. I was planning to escape also, not worrying about the Mini too much, when there was a clearing of people from behind the little car and a youth brought a heavy object smashing down on its rear window, which went opaque.

There are some things you can run from, others you can't. It's a fine moral line and I'm often not too sure where it is drawn with me, but somehow I was now involved. I pulled out the ignition key, used it on a glove locker and got my fingers around the butt of a Luger. I then stepped out on to hot asphalt.

The driver was also out of the Mini. It looked as though she had been pulled out. She was European, had almost white blonde hair, and seemed young. That was all I could see before the crowd closed in again. Through the shouting came a girl's voice, clear and sharp and in English:

'Leave me alone, you bastards!'

I took a crisis risk, raised the gun in the air and pulled the trigger. The Luger made a noise like a heavy door slammed. The crowd seemed to experience a sharp deflation of its first impulse towards corporate violence. Yowling quietened. Everything held, with attention switched down the road to me.

These were young men, youths mostly, and Malay. They were Moslems, which meant that there shouldn't have been a place in their faith for a worship of Kali, the Destroyer, but they had made room for her. The many-armed Hindu Queen of Hell was hostess on a hot afternoon. She likes an orgasmic spurting of blood at her really big parties.

The blonde was free of hands, standing alone, almost at the centre of a three-quarters circle of youths holding back more youths. None of the ones in front fancied martyrdom to a Luger bullet. It was too soon for the hysteria that could push a surge of boys towards a man with a gun.

The girl was wearing orange slacks. A white shirt had

been half-ripped from one arm. Her hair fell straight to her shoulders except for a strand across one eye. The other eye was a startling colour, the blue of African violets. She could be someone's daughter out from Britain for a holiday.

I walked perhaps a dozen paces up the road, then said to the girl:

'Get in my car.'

She didn't seem troubled about just abandoning the Mini, though she was very far from panic, coming towards me at just the right pace, not too fast. It looked as though she had some experience of tight situations and it would take more than a riot mob of youths to make her lose her cool.

She put up a hand and pushed back hair. I got a look from two astonishing eyes. At once, without really seeing the rest of her face, my mind registered her as beautiful. A moment later a door of the Mercedes clonked shut, that sound loud in a silence still so intense that the noise of traffic continuing to move in other parts of the city reached us.

I turned and walked back to the car watched by the girl through the windscreen. Shouting started, but it seemed to be coming from the rear of the crowd, the youths up front continuing to hold to discretion. I opened the driver's door, got in, and tucked the Luger by my thigh. I had to take the ignition key from the compartment lock to start the car and saw a movement in the crowd as I did this, a mass impulse coming like a wave from the back.

'Thanks,' the girl said.

'Wait till we're out of here.'

I couldn't quite make the U-turn in the large car, and had to reverse back. We were rushed. What I saw in the driving mirror wasn't pleasant, distorted faces and raised arms. A battering began on the boot. Voices caught a chant. Something hit a window. I got into drive again and we surged away.

'What are they shouting?'

'Kill the pig-eaters.'

'Why pigs especially?'

'It's usually kept for Chinese. I hope you get your Mini later.'

'To hell with that, it's rented.'

There was a minor side street ahead, not much more than a lane, but I knew I could get the car down it. I had the right-turn flashers on when a lorry came out from our escape passage pushing straight across the street to block both up and down traffic. There wasn't room behind it, either, to squeeze the Mercedes into the turn. I braked.

The lorry had a load in its open back, more youths, about thirty of them. These were equipped with sharpened bamboo poles held up like spears. They looked like reinforcements for a medieval war being rushed to the front in modern transport. The riot was about as spontaneous as deliberate arson.

On an order I didn't hear they began to jump down on to the roadway, holding those poles erect as they did it, trained in the manoeuvre. I looked in the mirror. The crowd had stopped almost on a line fifty yards up the road, turned audience for a new development. I put the Mercedes in reverse and steered over into the up lane, braking between two of the parked cars. What we were doing now didn't seem to interest the mob at all, it had suddenly become an inert, almost purposeless mass waiting to be activated by a catalyst.

The men from the lorry marched up the street in a shapeless crocodile following a leader distinguished by a white sweat band around his forehead.

'We get out,' I said.

'You're just leaving *this* car?'

'Better chance on our feet. Come on, slide over to my side.'

'Those pole vaulters can cut us off on the pavement.'

'They heard my gun.'

I kept the door open while the girl got out and slipped between the parked cars, then closed it, and lifted the Luger in my right hand, holding it out from my body to advertise that ours was an armed neutrality.

I joined the blonde on the pavement. We walked down the street as the storm troopers came up it, drawing level with no acknowledgement from either party. Then a big van hid us.

'They're just kids,' the girl said.

'These days you stop being a kid at fifteen.'

'Where are the police?'

'I'm not really expecting to see them. They're Malay controlled.'

'This is anti-Chinese?'

'Yes. That's why we're being allowed to walk out. I hope.'

The next to the last shop before the lane was fitting its last shutter under an awning, a woman doing the job and pretty frantic about it. Then she popped under cover, but before that final panel slammed a customer was ejected through it, hands pushing. It was a Tamil girl. She stood under that awning staring first up the pavement, then out into the road. She had been urbanized out of her sari into a cotton tartan mini skirt and pink blouse. From one hand dangled a white bag; she held the other arm tight in to her body. Above a starched neck frill her chiselled, tightly boned face was very black. Her people weren't the target for today but they could become this at any time, and if that happened youth wouldn't shield her, nor her sex. She was rigid, centred in that fear with which she had grown up, of a pogrom, of the majority turning against her particular minority.

From some impulse entirely beyond reason the girl jerked into movement, coming up the pavement towards us, and at a run, the white bag flapping. The idea could be to end isolation, to lose herself in the crowd up there. I didn't think she'd lose herself, the Malays don't love Tamils much either. She didn't seem to see us at all. I turned aside to grab a thin, bangled wrist.

The storm troopers reached the mob, fertilizing it. There was an immediate bellowing that covered the Tamil's wails as she struggled. The white handbag dropped to the pavement, its contents spilling out. I put the Luger in a jacket pocket.

'Get her into the lane,' I said. 'I'll pick up this stuff.'

The blonde took over with a woman to woman approach to hysteria, giving the weeping girl a stinging slap on one cheek. The Tamil allowed herself to be led away. I bent down to shove things into the bag, picking up everything

12

that seemed to matter though there had been a wide scattering of small objects.

There was the heavy crash of plate glass. I didn't have to turn my head to know whose window that was. Action had started at Mr Foh's.

I tucked the bag under my arm and followed the girls. They rounded the corner just as I reached the awning. I went under its shadow and stopped. A couple of hundred yards back the looting had started, portable radios already travelling from hand to hand. A passage was made for a man staggering under the weight of a twenty-four-inch television. The crowd's mood had undergone swift change, to a kind of frenzied merriment. A boy was dancing up and down on the pavement, a private celebration.

I could just see the roof of my car. Two heads bobbed about it, a couple of the troopers. They seemed to be opening all four doors and suddenly they dashed away up the road. A third man followed them from the rear of the Mercedes, running even faster.

There was an explosion that could have been a five-hundred pound bomb hitting cement. Flames shot thirty feet in the air, straight up. A great gout of jet smoke followed them. I had put fourteen gallons in the Mercedes's tank in the morning and it wouldn't be long before my car was nothing more than twisted metal. Heat could set off other tanks, too.

I ran for the corner. There were still quite a few people about in the lane but shutters were going up fast. A Chinese youth glared at me, then snapped to a metal grille, disappearing behind a door with a steel shield mounted over it. The place was a jeweller's. The girls were waiting for me against a wall. The Tamil snatched her bag, groped through it, then cried out in English :

'My purse! You didn't get my purse!'

'It must have rolled into the gutter.'

'Then I go . . .!'

'You're not going back for it. Neither am I.'

We had to hold her. She was making a noise again.

Across the lane shutters were being pushed into steel runners over the front of a cavern that until a few moments ago had been offering cotton fabrics printed in Japan. A fat man was doing the job, repelling refugees at the same time. People were suddenly wanting out of that lane fast, and I saw why. Another lorry with a load of pole-bearers was coming down it, slowly. It didn't seem a good idea to try to work our way past that one, even with a Luger to wave. We'd be in spear range doing it.

The fat man saw us coming.

'No selling, no selling! I shut!'

'Not yet,' I said.

I held him against a shutter to let the girls into the shop. He kicked me on the shins, then went limp. I moved into gloom and the fat man deepened this almost at once with the last board, slamming it into place and ramming home a bolt.

'What was that explosion?' the blonde asked.

'My car.'

'Oh, my God!'

'They're only kids,' I said.

Faint light came from an inner room. Where we were, long strips of cloth hanging from the ceiling gave the feel of behind scenes in a theatre from which everyone has gone home, leaving the place to its ghost. Then another boom set small objects tinkling and there was shouting from the back premises.

We went through a half-curtained arch into a place lit by one naked bulb. It was occupied by four plump Chinese matrons, two youths obviously assistants, and a round-faced girl in a tropic trouser suit with magenta paeonies splashed all over it. The ladies were clearly customers who had chosen the wrong day to go shopping and the girl could be the owner's daughter. She was certainly calm enough, sitting on a stool smoking, with one leg laid over the knee of the other, ignoring us and apparently untroubled by riots. But the matrons had a lot to lose in civic disorders and were easing the worry of that with ear-splitting Cantonese noise. This died down as we came in.

It was pretty clear that we weren't welcome. Europeans get blamed by all parties in times like these and the Chinese ladies had been carefully brought up to hate Tamils. They concentrated their stares on the Indian girl, who now stood perfectly still in front of a huge, dragon-lurid calendar, looking like an age-darkened statue of Our Lady of Sorrows.

It is the fragility of most Tamils which appeals to whatever protective instinct I have. Those small, moulded heads, fine bones, delicate hands, give them the air of having been brought into a world against which their only real protection is skin pigment. Hard sun doesn't harm them but almost anything else can, and they move as though with a deer's constant readiness to run, and fast, from the strong and the terrible.

'Do we just wait here?' the blonde asked.

'No. There's bound to be a back way out. These places are warrens.'

The proprietor heard me.

'You come,' he said. 'I show.'

The three of us followed the fat man into a long narrow room in which a light burned. The air reeked from what I took to be yesterday's joss offering to the family gods, then recognized as mosquito-repellent smudge. A single window was shuttered. The place was a kitchen with an electric cooker and a sink. It was bleak, furnished with only a few stools about a scrubbed table. The décor was trade posters gummed on to walls from which a greenish wash was peeling. In one corner, tucked back into shadow, was a raised platform made of cement which looked as though it had been inspired by the north Chinese *kang*, which is a dung-fired stove with a broad, flat top. Up on that top senior members of the family used to spend a considerable portion of their days warming away rheumatics and the very aged rarely climbed down at all, waiting for death in comfort.

This adaptation for the tropics was also occupied, no fire beneath, but with an old woman bundled in black up on it, her head pillowed on a padded wooden block. Light glistened from her open eyes but she gave no sign of seeing us. In one ear was a piece of jade, a little trophy from living still retained, but otherwise she was anonymous, and if sentient at all, concerned only with private journeys back down time spent. In Singapore the old lady might well have

15

been doing her waiting in a death house, and by her own request, but apparently the shop-owner was a sentimentalist who believed in keeping the family bones beside him until they were finally ready for interment.

The geriatric ward is one of the more unpleasant by-products of our time. This arrangement, pathetic as it was, still held a humanity of sorts. They had built the old lady a platform like the ones she remembered from the long-ago China of her youth and on which she had probably seen her grandmother die. A veteran was set to one side, but only just beyond routine bustle, able to hear the sounds of this for as long as she could hear anything. I warmed to the shop-owner.

He didn't warm to me. A final door was kept open only long enough to let us through. We stood blinking in sunlight, a noise of violence baffled away by buildings, like a sound track turned low.

'What now?' the blonde asked.

'We walk. No taxis.'

The Tamil girl started off on her own, sandals clicking. I ran after her, with two twenty-dollar notes in my hand.

'For your purse,' I said, holding them out.

She stared at the notes, then lifted her head. She spat in my face.

In spite of those wobbling sandals and a flapping bag she ran like an animal whose only defence is the quick get-away.

Western man does very little walking in Oriental cities, he never has, there was always some form of transport available and back in those days when local labour was really cheap he invented the rickshaw, a human puller being that much more economical to run than a horse. It isn't generally realized that the rickshaw was a Western idea, but it was, the first one designed by an Englishman in Yokohama.

In his Shanghai my grandfather never walked. Before he owned his snub-nosed Morris he had a private rickshaw with personal coolie whom he paid about ten per cent more than the man would have averaged free-lancing. My grandmother had her own rickshaw too, plus coolie, which was handy for the shopping and the Mah Jong parties, and she hung on to this means of getting about long after the car was available, much attached to the last of her rickshaw boys who died at the advanced age for his calling of thirty-nine, from the usual occupational complaint : coughing his lungs out.

Walking had begun to feel like some kind of penance for the sins of my grandparents. My shoes were too thin for hot asphalt. I carried my jacket and was very near to taking off a soaking shirt. The girl wasn't looking like any ad for anti-perspirant, either. There aren't any sweat-stoppers for really active people in an equatorial climate.

The streets were empty, except for cats. Dogs howled in courtyards. Chinese charactered signs and banners in many colours issued invitations cancelled by the shut doors underneath. Locked cars looked as though their owners would never come out of hiding to claim them. Noise was to the north, almost distant, but it still held the threat of thunder that could circle and catch us.

A couple of solitary hikers through a contemporary purgatory didn't ease the burden of their pilgrimage by getting to know each other. Her name was Jean Hyde, she was married, lived in a suburb unfashionable for Europeans, and had been in Kuala Lumpur for five weeks. I didn't ask what she thought of our city, contenting myself with the facts that could have come from a credit card. I was seeing her home because someone had to and she hadn't suggested that this was unnecessary. She was only about five feet two but had a good stride, as though used to hitch-hiking across Europe on a lifted thumb. My impression was that any male trying to rape her in a pup tent would regret the attempt. I had shoved up an earlier estimate of her age from nineteen to twenty-three or four or even more.

'Got a cigarette? My bag was on the Mini's shelf.'

'I don't use them.'

'Oh.'

I was classified, a Mercedes owner who had given up smoking in a bid to enjoy my comforts for as long as pos-

17

sible. Her husband could be a new lecturer at the University, probably in history with a Marxist slant, an academic who didn't mix with neo-colonialists and hated their clubs.

We went past a huddle of shops into a street called Bukit Pirdah Road, packed housing in which it wouldn't be difficult to find cheap rooms shared with cockroaches and from which you really got to know the natives in spite of slight obstacles like the language barrier. It was an area new to me, I hadn't even driven through it, and was surprised when the tone of the street changed, becoming first Chinese middle class, then Chinese more than that. It was a long road and before we were half-way down it there were villas on both sides set back in gardens, stopping places for pushing young executives on the way up to two acres of ground and a full-time night watchman. Architectural style tended towards that tropic rococo once seen never forgotten, highly coloured in mauves, pinks and yellows. The gates began to be impressive, offering tantalizing glimpses of just how well a considerable proportion of Malaysia's pushing minority are doing for themselves. I didn't think too much of the locale as a place in which to ride out the present turbulence, it seemed to offer a positive invitation for a visit from one of the motorized Malay riot units.

'This is where we camp,' Jean Hyde said.

The garden was tidily maintained and there was a drive through it leading to a two-storey façade above a formal terrace. There were palm trees sprouting out of urns. The place was bound to have at least ten rooms and in a city with an acute housing shortage was a very desirable property indeed. I knew of at least three families who spent all their spare time looking for something like this to rent or buy. Lucky Hydes with the right connections.

I shut wooden gates.

'What's the point of that, Mr Harris?'

'It slightly discourages callers.'

'You think trouble could spread out here?'

'It could spread anywhere today. Call your husband now. I'm staying until he comes back.'

She smiled.

'We'll have time to get to know each other. He's away for at least two weeks. Let's start with a long drink.'

We went up steps to the terrace. Her keys had been in the lost bag and she had to ring. The man who opened the door seemed an unlikely member of the local servants' union which is making things increasingly difficult for employers. He wore the right clothes, but looked burly in them, like an ex-pro boxer pretending to be a barman. If he had heard of the rioting against his race brothers and was worried about it, this didn't show. Jean treated him with the kind of polite reserve which said at once that there had been a nanny in her nursery despite the socialism that was by then starting to batter Britain, which cast doubts on my theory of a Marxist husband.

'I'm having a shower,' she said. 'You can have one, too, if you like. We've three bathrooms. And I could let you have a shirt of John's.'

'Can I phone my office first?'

'Certainly, if you can get through. It's in there. Fung will show you where to go after.'

The sitting-room was beyond an arch and I went into it feeling the chill of air conditioning on pores that have been opened. The place was lush but I couldn't name the period. The central arrangement was of chairs and a settee in teak with ventilated rattan bottoms. The big feature was the lamps, all identical, four undesirable nude ladies holding up their arms in a bid to retrieve pink silk crinolines that had somehow got whipped up over their heads. On the walls were views of the country I had seen before, the artist originally commissioned for poster work by Malaysian Railways. A big sidepiece was Chinese creative imagination gone mad over a hunk of black deadwood. There was also a roll-topped desk in one corner with the ridged flap lifted and the telephone was there. I dialled and at once got my secretary.

'Mr Harris! We've been worried stiff about you.'

'That's nice to hear, Maria. I've been worried stiff about myself.'

'Did the rioting stop you from getting here? You weren't caught in it?'

'Well, more or less. I'll tell you later. Is Bahadur about?'

'Yes. You want me to get him?'

'In a minute. How are things with you?'

'There's been nothing near us. But there is a fire just down from Batu Road.'

'Not much evidence of the police yet?'

'I really don't know. We've just been sitting here waiting to hear from you.'

'Listen, Maria, get your husband to collect you and go home. Have you heard from him?'

'Yes. There's nothing out our way yet. You're not coming to the office?'

'I may, but I won't need you. What I want now is Bahadur to get a car somewhere and come to collect me.'

'What's happened to the Mercedes?'

'Out of service. I'm at 127 Bukit Pirdah Road. Get Bahadur on to that, will you?'

'All right, Mr Harris. You look after yourself.'

I put the receiver back on its hooks. At one corner of the desk, neatly strapped with a rubber band, was a pile of unopened mail, mostly airletters, the top one made exotic with a Middle Eastern stamp. The address was:

'John Hyde, Esq.,
  c/o The Min Kow Lin Corporation,
    27-35 Itang Road,
      Kuala Lumpur,
       Malaysia.'

The Corporation were big in tin mining, very big, and a number of other things as well.

Fung was waiting in the hall. He took me up to a bedroom. I had the feeling he resented an order to put out one of John's shirts.

Jean Hyde had legs tucked up on to her chair. She was smoking, with one hand around a well fortified orange juice. It seemed unlikely that recent experience would have any traumatic effect on her personality. She was wearing black tights and another white shirt, her hair sleeked down on both sides of her face. She was a pretty girl, small nose, nice teeth, but if her eyes had been brown, or a utility blue, she'd have earned a moment's pause before you looked on for something more interesting. It was those eyes that could stop traffic and she knew this well, accenting them heavily with a boot-black surround.

'Like the pad in which I play memsahib? Unique isn't it? The owners had me expecting something rather different.'

This was conversational bait. I rose to it.

'Who are they?'

'A pair called Kwan and Mary Lee. We met them in Beirut. They got our flat and we got this.'

'You're on holiday?'

She nodded.

'Choose our times and places well, don't we? John has flair. Last time it was a peasant uprising in Peru.'

'As the wife of a geologist you get about.'

'Oh, clever Mr Harris. How did you guess geologist?'

'From a pile of professional journals in what I took to be your husband's bedroom.'

'Of course.'

'You don't stay together on holiday?'

'Hell, no. Or it wouldn't be. John has this thing about jungles, South America, Africa. He hadn't been in an Asian jungle at all. Just leaped at the chance. So we got on a plane. He's also a flora man. Botany is his second love. To me it's death. So I stay at base camp, which is this.'

'I'd have thought lonely for you. Why not get temporary cards for the clubs?'

Those almost purple eyes widened.

'Daddy believes in God and his clubs. That didn't rub off. I'm more interested in the living. What's behind the rioting?'

'Malay resentment of Chinese.'

'Is that the big thing?'

'Yes. And getting bigger.'

'I adore the Chinese. So civilized. Except when it comes to furnishing a house. Why don't the Malays like them?'

'They work too hard and make money. The Malays hate work and have no money. It creates a situation.'

'Chinese flash their rolls?'

'Somewhat. With things like this house. And Mercedes their favourite transport.'

'You're also competing, Mr Harris?'

'Yes.'

'I thought you looked that kind of bastard, if you'll forgive me saying so. Those boys in that mob . . . I'd have got away without you.'

'Pity I waited. It cost me a car.'

She did the eye widening act again.

'Tell me about those rioting boys.'

'They're a problem. They've poured into the cities from the villages. And with only a bad primary school education, if that. Our new democracy wasn't ready for them in such numbers.'

'So?'

'They're hungry. And now they're being organized.'

'We always reach the Red menace sooner or later. I've been living with it in Arabia. Every camel belongs to Moscow. Mix me another of these, will you?'

At the carved cabinet I said:

'You oughtn't to stay in this house alone tonight.'

'But I'm not alone. I've got Cook and Fung.'

'Chinese servants can just disappear in times of stress.'

'I don't think these ones will. But even if they do, I've got a little gun that shoots real bullets. And my hand doesn't wobble when I aim.'

I could believe that.

The phone rang. Jean Hyde went to the desk. She stood making approving noises into the instrument, then hung up and turned.

'The riots must be over. That was the police. They found my car and returned it to the hire company. The back window seems to be all that's wrong. My handbag was still in the tray. Apparently the money wasn't touched.'

She was a lucky girl.

CHAPTER II

I STAYED at my office until nearly eight, waiting for a phone call from London which finally came through. I walked home, taking two or three detours to avoid areas that sounded as though they were seeing action. I was near road blocks twice, but kept clear of them, getting out of a built-up area without being challenged. The suburb where the real money rests was cool and quiet, undulations of ground putting up earthwork insulation against any flare-ups of riot noise.

It was a long time since I had walked up my drive. The gradient is steep, an asphalt razor cut on a slope packed with jungle hardwoods that have the constant ministrations of tree surgeons, stethescoped for white ant nests and cleared of parasitic growths, even the little pale orchids which make themselves wells of rottenness in which to feed. Snakes which reach my antiseptic woods are killed and there isn't a stagnant pool anywhere in which mosquitoes can breed. Sometimes monkeys come on excursions from the adjacent public gardens to try out the long drops from high branches, but they never seem to stay long, as though the surrounding intense hygiene is too much for them. I wish they would set up a colony near me; I like them, they are a continuing and salutary rebuke to our pretensions. A dozen or so monkeys on a sunset lawn form an excellent diversion for a drinks party. Guests tend to go home early, feeling vaguely affronted.

My house is really a museum piece, a planter's bungalow from the late nineteenth century, an anachronism and becoming more so every year with the high rise buildings shooting up, not to mention the University's new glittering semi-Islamic domes on the horizon. I bought it as a near ruin and was at once plunged into an affair of the heart. Contractors have been after me for the site ever since, there is room for four blocks of luxury flats with penthouses.

I moved to Kuala Lumpur when it became the capital of

23

a new federation that was to include Singapore, and on the principle that where the politicians are concentrated is where the really strong trade winds blow. Now that Singapore has opted to go it alone I ought to live down there again but can't bring myself to do it even though trying to operate half my business within Lee Kwan Yew's new little empire from a base outside it offers some sharp obstacles. Not the least of these is the increasing bitterness between Chinese and Malays. A man attempting to keep a shoe in both camps finds it slippery underfoot.

Russell Menzies had put on all the lights. He doesn't contribute towards the housekeeping so doesn't mind the bills. He got into the habit of keeping bright light all around him when he was head of undercover British Intelligence in Singapore, considering it a prophylactic against surprise assassination. Even in retirement as my guest he takes no unnecessary risks and wears a Colt in bed, uncomfortably, tucked into the breast pocket of his pyjama jacket.

I couldn't see the city from the drive, just a red glow in the sky and I didn't look at that. I went up on to the verandah outside the sitting-room and tried one of the glazed french windows which were fitted when air conditioning was installed. It was locked. I knocked.

Russell took his time about coming. I half-expected the Colt to be in his hand, but it wasn't; he heaved into view amidst brightness making a target a gunman couldn't have missed even if his hand had been palsied. Russell is shaped like an avocado fitted with legs. As the window opened my dog began to bark beyond a closed door.

'I didn't hear any car,' Russell said.

'How could you, with television on?'

'There isn't any picture, just that music.'

It was martial music.

'I've been listening to the radio. Ten minutes ago they announced a curfew from nine pm. I rang the office about an hour ago, but couldn't get through.'

'The line was open for a trunk call.'

I walked over to the drinks tray and poured a small whisky. A sound of springs told me that he had settled again in his chair.

24

'You wouldn't see any of the rioting?'

'A little.'

'What happened?'

'They burned my car,' I said, and turned.

Russell never admits to surprise, total facial control part of his training. All he did was let out an atom cloud of smoke from rank Java leaf.

'The Mercedes?'

'That's right. We've only got the Mini left.'

'Into which I cannot get.'

'You're going to have to stretch your budget for taxi fares.'

'What about insurance?'

'I haven't found out yet whether Dale Mostin bought me cover for war and civil disturbance risk. I rather suspect he didn't.'

Russell stared.

'Are you saying that you're not going to get a replacement?'

'Probably something small. Like a Volkswagen.'

My partner couldn't get into them either. He looked at me without love.

'What actually happened to you?'

'Well, I waved a gun, then ran.'

I sat down and sipped the whisky. He watched me. After a moment he said with great perception:

'You've had a shake.'

A picture came on TV, not our usual announcer. The man said first in Malay, then English, that normal programmes would be resumed at nine o'clock. It was a great comfort to know that a Western with dubbed dialogue would be pushed out on the air as usual, but the man rather spoiled the effect of this by repeating the news of a curfew and saying that looters would be shot at sight. The screen went blank for a moment before giving birth to a printed notice telling us when to expect normalcy.

'The police will soon quieten this down,' Russell said.

I was certain that he hadn't left his chair all afternoon even to walk to the edge of the lawn for a view of the fires.

'The police weren't much in evidence. It was Malays

against Chinese. Organized, too. About as dirty as you can get.'

'Thinking of emigrating, are you? Back to our native Scotland? It was clever of you to make those arrangements for your exit pass, a business in the old country.'

'If you could call it a business. It's practically bankrupt. There'll be no dividend this year or next and I certainly couldn't live in Scotland on my director's fee.'

He reached for one of the cans of beer beside him, opened it by its patent zip top and poured the contents carefully into a glass already carrying froth stains.

'None the less there's a way out for you, Paul. Just what would make you bolt from Malaysia?'

'A reasonable certainty that I'd have my throat cut if I didn't.'

I got up and went along to my room, fought off the welcoming Tosa hound, had a shower and changed into a dressing-gown. Taro came back to the sitting-room with me. The dog won't ever stay alone with Russell, and makes it pretty plain that he thinks my giving an old man house room was a great mistake.

'When do you want to eat?' Russell asked.

'I'm not hungry.'

'It's South African rock lobster tails from cold storage. I thought we might have a hock.'

He would play the gourmet right up to the day of his funeral. I had another whisky and sat down with it.

'Russell, can you think of any reason why the Min Kow Lin Corporation would import an oil geologist from the Persian Gulf?'

He looked at me.

'What makes you think they have?'

'I was caught in the riot with the geologist's wife. She claims they're on holiday. Somehow I find that difficult to believe. Do you know if Min have ever gone in for oil searches?'

'I couldn't say off hand. What's this geologist's name?'

'Hyde. They have a house in a Chinese suburb. Found for them, obviously. Nicely tucked away from other Europeans. I get the feeling the isolation is deliberate.'

'Min Kow Lin policy?'

'Yes. And I'd almost bet it's part of their contract with Hyde. The man is away in the jungle at the moment, allegedly collecting plant life. His wife's story was raw right through, it needed a lot more cooking. And I keep wondering why it was hastily served to me.'

'How did you find out about the Min connection?'

'Hyde's mail on a desk was addressed through them.'

After a moment Russell said:

'A geologist could have two specialities, one of them tin.'

'That's why I phoned our London agent. Hyde has been in oil all his life, and he's good. Makes big money.'

'It's not inconceivable that Min could be joining our local oil rush. A lot of people are doing it. Had you heard the sea rig off Singora claims a strike?'

'No. Is it going to be commercial?'

'I doubt it. The company's shares jumped two dollars and sixty-three cents yesterday. I phoned my broker to get rid of my holdings, I've been waiting for the right moment to unload. Out of every twenty-five strikes we hear of in the next few years twenty-four will be duds.'

Russell stood and trundled out of the room. I knew where he was going. He had brought up with him from Singapore half a ton of files, a by-product of forty years of complex living. These must once have been kept under conditions of considerable security but they were now housed in a vast mahogany bookcase in his bedroom protected by a lock I could have sprung with a piece of bent plastic. I'd thought more than once about doing this but somehow the right opportunity had never presented itself. The old man did a lot of his living in that bedroom and was rarely away from the house except in my company.

He once admitted that there were more than sixty thousand mini dossiers of people and companies packed into those folders though he insisted that the contents were now only of historical interest, already irrelevant in the swift changing contemporary situation. I had my doubts about this. It seemed to me possible that the records were being regularly up-dated. For one thing Russell did a lot of hunt and peck typing on a small portable, far more than could be accounted for by his outgoing mail; for another, that activity quite often became most marked the day after we had one of our increasingly celebrated dinner parties which always had me at the dull end of the table. Russell's taste in guests was catholic provided everyone invited had a success story behind them, and this tended to be a political or commercial story. Never seen were any kind of academics, even scientists, whose importance in our time my partner says is grossly exaggerated. Civil servants also, except a few at the very top, didn't sit down to those carefully thought-out menus and we had no contacts at all amongst the clergy, Christian, Mohammedan, or Hindu.

Trying as I find the old man most of the time I know perfectly well that he has his function in my business. His experience is encyclopedic, including a deep understanding of commercial law as it is practised in South East Asia. He could have made a fortune as a corporation lawyer but instead had chosen to squander talent in a way that had seemed positively perverse, even going to the extreme of appearances in court on behalf of petty thieves. I used to think this was because he wasn't really interested in money, only beer, but it turned out to be all part of the web he needed to spin about his central undercover role.

Russell arrived back in the sitting-room, but not carrying a file; he never flaunted these in front of me.

'In 1958 Min Kow Lin had twenty square miles of oil exploration area all staked out at Tanjong Selor in North Borneo. Then Sukarno expropriated. Compensation was derisory and never paid. Wells were sunk and six of them have come in since, administered by the Indonesian state combine.'

'Min were cheated,' I said.

'Quite.'

'Have they tried for oil anywhere else?'

'It's not on my records.'

He came over to his chair, sat, and opened another can of beer. Apparently he had forgotten all about lobster tails. In a Zen withdrawal, and staring again at a wall, he looked like a Buddhisattva grown fat from sedentary contemplation, only needing to unveil his navel.

I didn't know whether he was thinking about oil, but I was. It has taken a terrible toll on this century. If the Japanese had possessed plenty of their own there's a fair chance there would never have been a Pearl Harbour. And the thing I particularly dislike about the stuff is the way it always seems to be discovered in backward areas, practically overnight destroying the traditional patterns in these places and imposing instead a kind of chaos from too much money too fast.

Malaysia, of course, is far from a backward area, with her rubber and tin, and though encircled by oil wells from Sumatra via Borneo right around to new workings in southern Thailand just across our one land frontier, the slime hasn't yet been found in commercial quantities on the peninsula. It's almost as if nature had said you've got enough, you don't get this, and I've always been perfectly happy to go along with that ruling. A number of other people are not and keep up the search, refusing to believe that we don't have what our neighbours do.

It looked as though Min Kow Lin had taken up this game again. They are a corporation with enormous capitalization, the parent company in Singapore, but with practically autonomous subsidiaries in Malaysia, the Philippines, Cambodia and Thailand. With us its policies have recently been a rationalization, via centralized control, of both tin mining and rubber estates and for years now I've been watching them buy up independent rubber plantations and take over smaller Chinese syndicates. I've never actually come into open conflict with them and one reason for this could be my discretion, for compared to Min Kow Lin my company is just a minnow to a shark, and in swallowing me they wouldn't even notice the taste. At the same time I had reason not to like them much.

Russell switched his gaze from a wall to me.

'You planning something?' he asked.

'Yes.'

'What?'

'To find out where John Hyde is and why. Mrs Hyde was terribly vague about whether the jungle her husband is in lies to the north, south, east or west. And I'd have said she was a girl with a very sharp sense of direction.'

'This woman seems to have impressed you.'

'Oh, she did.'

'I don't see why Min's search for oil, if that's what it is, should concern us? You've always said that the oil business stinks.'

'It would stink worse under Min's capitalization. If they should find the stuff they'd exploit it entirely by and for themselves. They have the resources to do that, to form an oil subsidiary and bring in the technicians they need to run it, including building a refinery.'

'Well?'

'Russell, you know perfectly well what I'm getting at. With Min getting their claws into this it would be to hell with any benefits from what is a national natural resource flowing towards Malays.'

'There would be the tax revenues.'

'Sure, on Min's declared income after brilliantly designed fiddles. That's going to mean only a fraction of the oil take reaching the Malay majority. But if the State was in on this from the ground floor things could be very different.'

'Fancy Paul Harris advocating a nationalized industry!'

'I'm not. Just a consortium in which Malay interests have the casting vote, not Chinese interests.'

'If our respected government smell oil in Malaysia they'll be in on it.'

'I'm not too sure about that. All Min has to do is request a concession for tin mining and then see that the contract includes all mineral rights. That's routine anyway. I believe they could have the oil thing swinging before the government could step in.'

'What have you got against Min personally?'

I didn't try to lie to Russell, it never does any good.

'Some years ago when I was badly stretched to finance our shipping company the word got around Singapore that Harris and Company was on the point of going bust. That word was put around by Min, who meant to have me for breakfast.'

'How do you know?'

'A Chinese director of Johore Diesels told me. He was worried. He believed it.'

'So it's a vendetta?'

'I'm not as ambitious as that, I'd just like to put a stick between spokes if that's at all possible.'

'You've been talking about a Malay dominated consortium if there is oil. Where do we fit into that?'

'As part of the consortium.'

'All I can say to that is you're stark staring mad. Your geologist may very well be looking for botanical specimens.'

'I have a hunch he isn't.'

'Your hunches were always bringing you near liquidation before I officially came into the firm. Let me raise one little practical point, Paul. Supposing there is oil and you put the Malays wise to this, which I assume is your idea, just how do you set about forming that consortium?'

'I do it through Batim Salong.'

'*What*? That playboy!'

'He's a cousin of the ruling house and has the ear of everyone who matters in the Malay community.'

'What's the good of having ears available if you never whisper into them? Salong could have been Prime Minister if he'd wanted to stir himself off his behind, but he didn't, and he never will.'

'He's a highly intelligent man.'

'The obituary notice of ninety per cent of the world's failures.'

'I can prod him.'

'What with?'

'His hatred of the Chinese.'

'So you're going in for local politics after all?'

'No.'

Russell glared.

'Look, boy, you're standing with one foot in each camp as it is. At any time it could be the splits, with you coming down on your balls. If you step back on the Malay side openly in something like this the Chinese will mass to get you. And that's one kill I don't want to witness.'

31

'You could resign your directorship and move to an hotel.'

He upended a beer can and a few drops dribbled into his glass.

'I'm fortunate in my old age,' he said. 'My mission has stayed with me. To keep you from making a bloody fool of yourself. And I've been at it since you were in short trousers. I thought I could do the job and be semi-retired at the same time, but it seems not. On the evidence available, which is nil, you are not justified in taking any action on this matter.'

'I'll collect the evidence before I take action.'

'Oh, God!' Russell said. 'Let's eat.'

The television set, left switched on, replaced a printed promise with a face. It was our usual announcer back again and from the look of him he was about to read the news, which was all bad. The government had panicked and declared martial law, suspending the constitution. Mobs were out in the streets again and new fires had started. The curfew would be strictly enforced. The police had orders to shoot to kill, which meant shoot to kill Chinese.

'So much for one man, one vote,' Russell said. 'Not that it ever meant a damn here. Or ever means a damn anywhere. We now have a dictatorship. Maybe you can believe it will be benevolent, I can't.'

'If the Chinese are going to be under restraint it could be a good time to start a Malay backed project.'

He looked at me.

'You won't die in bed, Paul.'

I went down on to the lawn in a dressing-gown while Taro ran on ahead, doing a quick check of our perimeter. I saw him pause to sniff the air, as though our atmosphere offered a difficult to identify scent this morning.

I couldn't smell anything out of the ordinary and under early light the city didn't look too badly marked. There were some gaps amongst the packed three-storey buildings in the central shopping streets but no smoke rose from these and they suggested extractions more than anything else, as though some giant, maniac dentist had been at work with a forceps. The high rise towers still shone and the plated domes of learning positively glittered. There was some traffic in the roads and an optimist could have seen a return to norm down there.

Breakfast was waiting on the main verandah and so was our houseboy. While I was in Europe my old faithful dug up the ancient excuse of sick relations and left, in my view because he didn't much like the permanent company I was keeping at home. Russell had found Soo Chong as a replacement. The man is tall for a Chinese and very thin. He wears a white Nehru jacket over black cotton jeans and has the gaunt look of someone who has long shared his living with a tape worm. After our first meeting I insisted that he be hospitalized for this highly contagious complaint, which he was for two days, but Chong hasn't fattened up at all since. Traces of smallpox, rare these days, sit on both his cheeks, and though he still moves like a youth, I'm convinced he's in his seventies and his history probably includes being with Mao Tse-tung on the Long March. However, the man's highly efficient if not immediately lovable. Also, he knows I pay the bills and is as polite to me as he is to Russell, which is something.

In areas of the world where servants are still part of the social pattern it's as well to be thankful for this and not worry much about whether they like you. The answer is almost certainly that they do not and can even be that given the right circumstances they would cut your throat with a certain zest. I expect my dog to love me but not my cook.

I sat down to find that the dish chosen for my breakfast on the first day of martial law was rather a subtle one . . . scrambled eggs. I poured coffee and looked at the view. I do this not for inspiration but for perspective, which usually comes at once. As far south as we are the country's main spine isn't really much more than jungle covered hills and from twenty miles away these look sweetly innocent, green tones gently changing under altered light. In fact half a mile from the tarmacadam highway through the nearest pass a man can wander in circles until he dies. Only a few months back tourists parked a hired car in a sylvan glade and went down what seemed to be a path to get some views of raw nature with their Leicas. The car was picked up by a police patrol within hours, but a two-day search didn't even come up with a piece of Hawaiian shirt. Our papers didn't play this up because the locals knew what had happened, the pair had quickly exhausted themselves making a noise and finally dropped to the ground under that airless green covering. Panthers had found them.

Anything can be under those endless green forests, or nothing much, and surveys from the air show very little. Low flying small planes are subject not only to sudden and very violent electric storms but also a static defence of heat thermals which can take a light aircraft and just shoot it up for a couple of thousand feet. If the pilot loses consciousness during that ascent the drop again tends to be fatal. Even helicopters haven't helped too much, a number of them have just disappeared in the high ranges to the north.

Malaysian jungle sits at the edge of what man has taken from it waiting to return, ready when resistance has gone again to come sweeping across paddy to swallow the domes and the glass towers. Even an atomic blasting would see the jungle still alive and ready for some mutated comeback.

I had my perspective on an oil search; it would be madness to waste any time snooping after Min Kow Lin. As so often, Russell was right. Then he came through a window from the sitting-room looking pleased with himself as he often did in the mornings and suddenly the project was on again.

Russell was wearing a pyjama top without Colt and in place of bottoms, probably because he couldn't get into them, a green sarong. The outfit did even less for him than most of his other costumes.

'They're throwing pork into Malay *kampongs*,' he announced.

'Who?'

'Chinese hooligans. On the radio. Chinese gangs terrorizing Malays now.'

'Makes a change,' I said.

'They're saying the Chinese millenium has arrived. When they'll put down the Malays.'

'Government propaganda.'

A wicker chair creaked under him.

'I've been thinking, Paul.'

'I knew you would be.'

'If it does turn out there's something in what you've stumbled on I know how we can handle it.'

I shouldn't have been surprised, but I was, even though every now and then Russell does a complete about face, contriving in the process to make my ideas his own. He had already breakfasted from a tray by his bed but I poured him a cup of coffee. He lit his cheroot like a politician does a pipe, using the interlude for puffing to suggest the sober, thoughtful leader who never rushes his pronouncements but will stand by them to the end once he has.

'Paul, if there really is anything in what you've stumbled on then there is no alternative to bringing in one of the big oil companies.'

'Not at this stage,' I said.

He ignored me.

'Document whatever evidence we can collect, then you fly with it to Texas to contact Kenoco with an offer to be their man on the spot.'

'I'm not flying anywhere.'

He didn't seem to be hearing me at all.

'You're known, which would keep red tape to a minimum. I think Kenoco would move into this at once, using us as their agents on the spot. After all, they're gambling practically every day. On consideration I think your idea of using Batim Salong is probably sound enough, though he must be kept on the fringe, his job to steer concessionary rights, via us, to Kenoco. And as you say, he has the contacts. But it would be a mistake for him to know too much.'

'This was to be a big Malay thing,' I said.

Russell looked at me.

'Don't be a fool! Salong and his friends couldn't begin to put up the capital privately for a major oil exploitation. I doubt whether even the State could do it with the way things are now. Also, there's no oil know-how in this

35

country. That has to be imported, together with finance.'

'Agreed,' I said sweetly. 'But we wouldn't need to import anything for round one, the idea of that being to knock Min out of the picture. When that was done our consortium would have plenty of time to go shopping for outside finance. And in a seller's market. But all this is academic, Russell. I spent a practically sleepless night, too. As you pointed out any antagonizing of the Chinese community either here or in Singapore would be lethal to the interests of Harris and Company. So I'm going to show the kind of good sense you're always counselling and drop the whole thing. Forget about it. After all, we're doing all right. Record profits this year.'

He stared. I stood.

'Have you got anything for me to post on the way to the office?' I asked.

The Kuala Lumpur headquarters of Harris and Company are a small experiment in the potential for inter-racial harmony. My private secretary is half Portuguese of old Malacca stock to which has more recently been added a quarter of Chinese blood and another quarter of British. She is a tropic ex-beauty now on the fade into late thirties, overweight, married to a Tamil schoolteacher with two near adult children by his first wife. Maria has had enough faith in the future to have two more children by the Tamil, these now at their father's school. The Accountant is that generally untrusted mix . . . Chinese-Malay. Both my personal assistants are Indians, one a Tamil, the other a Sikh, the first good at desk work, the second preferring roving commissions for which he has real talent in spite of the fact that it is difficult to imagine anything less inconspicuous than a lean, erect figure six feet tall sporting a snow white turban and a jet black beard, these usually worn above a neat tropic business suit. Bahadur Singh has a law degree from Kuala Lumpur University and was making a reasonable living as a young solicitor articled to a firm in the city when I found him and persuaded him that the pickings would be better with me and the life more interesting. I haven't regretted my decision and I don't think he has.

We moved the office recently into a three-storey building vacated by a Chinese mining syndicate after its third lucky strike of tin. The place requires complete renovation and architects are working on the plans, but meantime we make do with creaking stairs, doors that shut the second time you kick them and electric fans sending hot draughts about the place. I looked into Maria's office. She had her usual serene smile for me.

'Good morning, Mr Harris.'

'Let's hope it will be. No trouble getting home last night?'

'None. It's quiet out our way. How's your hill?'

'If it weren't for television we wouldn't know there's a war on. Is everyone in?'

'All except the typist.'

'We can get along without her. You came in a taxi, I hope?'

'I used my bicycle as always.'

The family car takes Maria's husband and the kids to school while Mum sails forth on her ladies' model, with dropped central bar, that must have first been put on the road somewhere about the end of World War One. It has a vast shopping basket hitched on to handlebars in which she could take home her electric typewriter if she felt like it, and mounted on that machine Maria would intimidate police and any stray rioters who might still be about. The Mini had twice been stopped at roadblocks but it was my bet that no one had stopped Maria. I had seen her coming down crowded streets, weaving in and out amongst cars, and at her own pace, her progress a proclamation that Malaysia belongs to the Eurasians. It's a pity that more of them can't believe this and assert themselves, they could become an effective political force.

Maria's maternal instinct is ample enough to include me at its edges. She thinks I don't eat enough, drink too much and believes that she is really behind my final abandonment of the cigarette habit, still at work to get me off cigars as well. I asked her to summon Bahadur and then walked along to my own room, past the door to the office that was assigned to Russell when we moved and which he has only entered twice in nearly two years.

I sat down behind my desk knowing that Bahadur would take about two minutes to show up, and that he would knock once, sharply, then turn the handle and come in, whether or not invited to. The Sikh has a precise mind, he likes things defined, and from this worries about status quite a bit. Status is not something stressed too much in my office and on occasion Maria offers advice on top administration matters that might irritate a lot of employers. She and Russell don't get on too well, which may be why he doesn't come in more often. Bahadur's official rating is my number one personal assistant. He feels this is a ridiculous label in view of his responsibilities and his chance of becoming a co-director before too long is one of the things at the back of his mind all the time. But he is not getting on the Board yet. I made the mistake of appointing a too young director some years ago, with semi-disastrous results, and this time any new candidate is going to be subjected to a series of exhaustive tests. Bahadur would accept the need for these tests quite happily if in the meantime he was given a rank which at least came near to his own estimate of his value, but Personal Assistant to the Chairman is a kind of insult, even though it is never waved at him.

He knocked once, then turned down the handle. He didn't ask what I wanted of him, just took a seat. He looked ridiculously dignified for his twenty-seven years.

Bahadur neither drinks nor smokes. He isn't married and I've wondered about that. The Sikhs didn't start that old Oriental jingle about women for duty, boys for pleasure and melons for delight, but it still applies to a fair number of them. Bahadur hasn't got around to duty yet.

'I've an impossible proposition for you,' I said.

He didn't smile, even though he has teeth of his own as perfect as any dental plates. He listened to me, tugging his beard, a magnificent affair, solid, squared off black fibre slightly teased out at the bottom edge.

'Min Kow Lin,' he said, when he had heard me out. 'They're big.'

'And with tight security. Sensitive to threats of commercial espionage.'

'You want me just to go where this leads?'

'Not without telling me that you're leaving town. I think an anti-Chinese emergency might prove favourable to us. Panic loosened tongues and so on. Exploit this with a little payola and we may get some place.'

'You will authorize expenses with the Accountant?'

'I will. And I'll check on the government geological survey department myself. I'm not expecting a lead there but it's a flank that has to be covered. I know the man who runs the place and he'll let me see records. All surveys done by private companies are supposed to be filed.'

'I'll phone in as soon as I have anything, Mr Harris.'

'Do that. Incidentally, this is between ourselves. Even Mr Menzies doesn't know I'm taking any action on the matter.'

That pleased him. He almost smiled. Before he reached the door the phone rang. Maria's rich contralto came through.

'A Mr Potter to speak to you.'

This was a surprise. I'd have thought Archie Potter would have used the excuse of riots to stay clear of his office but it seems the whole world is adopting a business as usual slogan for these emergencies.

'Put him on.'

The connection took a moment or two. Archie's job is really a hangover from the days of the British Raj even though it didn't exist when the Union Jack waved over King's House. He is a commercial adviser to the Malaysian government. I'm pretty certain that soon the government is going to realize it doesn't need Archie, but meantime he sits in an office, or goes about the country with foreign delegations, killing time until he qualifies for a pension. The Potters are on Russell's entertainment list not because Archie is important, but because he is in frequent contact with people who are.

'Is that you, Paul?'

'It is. How do you like working for a dictatorship?'

'Hey! Not over the phone!'

'What's the matter? Have we got thought police on the job already?'

'For God's sake, man, watch it!'

There was a high degree of tension over in the corridors of power, which didn't surprise me.

'Are you free tonight?' Archie asked.

'Who's free in a curfew?'

'I was wondering if you'd come to dinner?'

'Are you sending an official car with an armed escort?'

'It's only the other side of the park. There's no trouble up our way.'

There are some houses offering a cuisine I'd break a new law for any day, but not the Potters. Russell says their cook started off life as a Hailam night soil carrier and hasn't been a learner.

'The thing is, I've got someone on my hands,' Archie said. 'A Japanese. He's down here selling tractors.'

'Not lucky in his timing.'

'You can say that again. Mr Akamoro is much cast down. He hasn't sold one. My job was to take him around, including Ipoh, but there's been rioting up there, too.'

'Why doesn't Mr Akamoro go back to Tokyo and try again later?'

'I don't know. I wish he would. Just now I can't even produce local businessmen for him to meet.'

'What's his firm?'

'Something called the Obori Agricultural Machine Company. But that's a subsidiary of something else.'

'Can you tell me what else?'

'Yes, I think so. Just a minute.'

There was a pause. Then Archie's voice.

'They're part of the Hawakami complex.'

I sat up straight. Another part of the Hawakami complex, the Tatsukeshi Marine Diesel Corporation has just taken from me the Manila franchise for my Johore engines. And by vicious, totally uneconomic price cutting. Hawakami, in fact, were out to kill me in one small area and if they succeeded would move on to others, possibly even Malaysia in due course. It was all a tiny part of Japanese expansion in that third of the world on which they mean to have a complete stranglehold by 1980.

'Paul, would you come? I'm sure Mr Akamoro would be interested to meet you. We've got some people staying . . . house guests. What a time for that, eh? And the Millsons are coming from next door.'

'I'll be there,' I said.

CHAPTER III

THE POTTER MANSION dates back to 1940 when Europe was at war but Malaysia hitting a high prosperity peak, the prices for rubber the fanciest they had ever been. A lot of lush houses were rushed up then, for no one really believed the Japanese were coming, including the generals who had been given the job of warding them off. The country planned to be a little oasis during world chaos, with everyone who held the right shares getting pretty rich. This had been my father's assessment of the situation and he paid the ultimate price for a wrong development forecast, dying in a Singapore internment camp.

The residences of those good old days which didn't last for very long tended to be built in poured concrete in a kind of tropic Spanish-American that had proved durable enough once the settling in cracks had been patched up. Ruth Potter has amused herself by compiling a history of her home which is in a sense a history of the country during three decades. In early 1943, after being looted and partially burned, it was converted into a high-ranking Japanese officers' brothel and had this function until liberation in 1945, when it was used for a year or two as offices for the British re-occupation army. It then reverted to private hands but in the civil war against the Communists, known as The Emergency, one of the few terrorist patrols that penetrated into Kuala Lumpur itself chucked a bomb through a window which meant considerable rebuilding and re-decoration. Since then it has only been burgled four times but Ruth has the feeling that it is scheduled for more exciting developments soon.

I thought of this as I walked up the tarmac drive. The place looked calm enough tonight, serene under the rising moon, perched on a hillock of mown jungle grass through which were dotted bougainvillaea and beds of cannas. The surviving Raj weren't showing many lights, being discreet about a party on a night when beyond that screen of the park there was still terror in fire-stained streets and people weeping behind shuttered doors.

In terms of the contemporary East it was something of a miracle that this house was still occupied by the kind of people who had built it, and of the same race. The British Empire is supposed to have ended with a whimper in the Fifties, but it can be argued that it didn't quite. Certainly there were a great many ceremonies of lowering the old flag for the last time at sunset, and the impressive uniformed figures disappeared, but in their place a new crop showed up, fairly hard workers most of them, engaged on campaigns to sell cars and agricultural machinery. There are almost as many Britons resident in India as there used to be under the Raj and Malaysia still has a surprising number too. It may be that the British will go down in history as the world's most adhesive people, able to stay fixed on surfaces too rough for most other racial glues.

I rang the bell. Ruth opened the door, on to semi-dark.

'Oh, Paul, marvellous you could come. Any trouble?'

'Some ducks in the pond protested and I saw a patrol car.'

'It didn't see you?'

'I was behind a tree.'

'What a time we live in.'

She said that as though she found it intensely interesting.

'You still have your servants?' I asked.

Ruth told me that her cook, poor fellow, had nowhere else to go, which didn't surprise me.

'We have the Winthrops up from Singapore,' she said in a whisper. 'All through this. It's been too ghastly. What does one do with house-guests in a riot? But it's all going to blow over soon, isn't it?'

'For the time being.'

'I refuse to be gloomy. Come along. Apologies for this creepy lighting. Don't trip over the edge of that rug. Bimbo gnaws it whenever we're out.'

The living-room was dimly lit too, so there wouldn't be a shine through curtains. Eyes turned towards the latest contact from the outside world.

'Paul walked all the way from his house,' Ruth said. 'Nothing happened.'

'And I had a perfectly normal day at the office,' I told them.

Mrs Winthrop, a gaunt woman accustomed to a quiet life under Lee Kwan Yew's firm administration, and shocked by this flare up on her holiday, looked at me with suspicion. Betty Millson, from the next house, didn't do much to reassure the visitors.

'Tom says it's not nearly over yet. And our phone went dead this afternoon, I mean really dead. As though it had been cut. It's like The Emergency again, isn't it? Not that I was here then.'

She meant that she had been a schoolgirl in those bad days, which wasn't quite the truth. I was taken over to meet a Japanese with a selling problem. Ruth called out:

'Archie, give Paul a great big whisky. He's not driving.'

Mr Akamoro accepted the introductions with much politeness, his glasses glinting as he bowed. He, too, had been given a great big drink, and there was a slight flush on his plump cheeks. He was not of the Yamato type which gets its aristocratic good looks from a Malay strain in the racial stock, but part of that major Mongolian flow into his islands which tends to round faces and a rather close concentration of essential features in the middle of them. He hadn't much nose, which meant that the earpieces of his glasses had to be hooked to hold them on. With those large black rimmed spectacles and slicked down hair his head was something of a study in circles, and as though to point this up his mouth went round almost every word he spoke, probably from elocution training which had insisted on a wide parting of the lips to let Western gutturals get clear.

'You are often visiting Japan, Mr Harris?'

'Not so frequently these days.'

'You do not enjoy?'

'Frankly, no. Your business efficiency scares me to death.'

He laughed. His teeth were slightly rounded, too.

'So? I think you flatter.'

'I wish I did. But I have a horrible feeling that we're never going to catch up with your head start. Every night I pray that rising Japanese living standards force your prices up, too.'

'In that case prayers most highly successful. This now happens. Only yesterday a motor car for factory worker does not come into mind. Now this man must have. Also colour television. Also modern kitchen. We are soon in your trap, Mr Harris.'

'Thanks for the encouragement on this dismal day.'

He went solemn.

'I am most sad for what happens here now.'

I looked into those spectacles. It was impossible to know whether he was speaking the truth. Archie brought me my whisky.

'Have you heard the latest Mao-think story from Hong Kong?' he asked.

'Yes,' I said. Archie told it anyway.

The dinner was like all Ruth's dinners. I have the feeling she cuts illustrations of fancy dishes out of women's magazines and shoves them at her cook, insisting that he try them first time on guests. She sat at her own table eating a succession of messes with every indication of relish, as bright as a nesting blackbird. Mr Akamoro, brought up to believe that it is the height of rudeness to leave anything when you are being entertained, practically scrubbed his plates, which is more than I did.

The Potters kept up the forms and the gentlemen stayed behind in the dining-room with good malt whisky for a bull session. Archie started it off with an outstandingly unfunny story about a colleague on leave visiting a London strip joint. Winthrop capped that with an account of how Singapore whores had carried on trading when a purity campaign closed down their brothels. As a piece of social documentary

44

this might have been interesting if I hadn't happened to know there wasn't a word of truth in what the man was saying. Through all this Mr Akamoro smiled, but contrived at the same time to leak the thought that the Western barbarians have about had their day and that it is time for Japanese initiative to take over with Zen Buddhism for the moral trimmings. I was tempted to lean over to the gentleman to point out that geisha parties are worse. For sheer vulgar barbarism Japanese public social life takes some beating and there isn't, in their patterns, the equivalent of our private social life. They may have a real point here, of course.

When we joined the ladies they had exhausted the topic of how ghastly it is for women in the Orient these days trying to run their homes with unreliable servants and were waiting for us. We mixed but somehow nothing jelled and Ruth, now with just a hint of desperation behind those smiles, tried to keep things going with the terrible game of living-room musical chairs which means that just as soon as you have got moderately comfortable, if not in spiritual communion with your partner, you're whipped away and planked down by someone else. I was shifted from Betty Millson to Mrs Winthrop, which was certainly going from bad to worse, for the lady from Singapore though by no means elderly, was set in the social vintage of 1928 which was a poor year to begin with and has since gone sour. In Mrs Winthrop's view South East Asia had never really been under proper control since the days when the Dutch planters over in Java used to go in for corporal punishment of rubber workers at morning muster. Mr Winthrop, for all his assumed good cheer, would have in his wife a very real commercial liability for the place and age in which he operated. Perhaps he kept her locked up most of the time.

In due course it was my turn for Ruth who arrived pretty exhausted and again whispering.

'There is absolutely no way to keep Clara Winthrop from coming to see you when she's decided to do that. But with the rioting we ought to be safer in future. And they're going home tomorrow, thank God. It's the Japanese

45

I'm worried about really. Archie was such a fool to insist on having him tonight. I mean with the curfew. Apparently he never thought about that. We simply can't drive the man back to his hotel. What do we do, ring for a police car? I'd give him a bed if we had one but with the Winthrops and the children that's impossible. Sometimes I could kill Archie, I really could. Anyway, I can't see why he has to help *Japanese* to sell tractors.'

'Your husband is a loyal servant of Malaysia's best interests.'

'Oh, is *that* what it is?' Ruth didn't smile.

About ten someone wanted to know what was happening out there in the dark and the television was switched on but it was showing a cheap rental British serial of low life in Liverpool, with Malay dialogue, mostly in falsetto, so Archie tried the radio. This was more with it, and not encouraging. Night had brought out the mobs again and new fires had been started. If the police were shooting at all it was over the heads of their race brothers.

'Oh, God!' Ruth said.

I told her that I would take the Japanese gentleman home for the night. I saw Mr Akamoro staring at me from across the room.

A sound of distant shouting stopped us by the duck pond. While we waited Mr Akamoro picked up a stick and puddled in the water with it, his face averted.

A considerable section of the park is still practically jungle and that's where the monkeys live, but the area in which we stood is groomed, the few monster hardwoods permitted to remain relieved of the need to struggle for sun and grown fat and sleek like burghers who calmly accept the easy comfort of their security as God's special gift to them. Each tree has its carefully tended support area of mown grass and pruned shrubs while above an immaculate tidiness was a night sky that might have been specially painted in by a Chinese hack artist, moon with attendant wisp clouds. The place now seemed to me an exercise in phoney peace, and I felt a sudden revulsion from an area in which I daily walked my dog and which I had accepted as an oasis reserved against the aggressive city. It no longer seemed that.

The shouting died away. A plane droned. We moved on.

'You haven't come to a very happy country,' I said to make some kind of noise between us.

'To be happy any place most difficult.'

'I'd have thought Japan offered a good chance to her native sons.'

He looked at me. The half circles of his eyebrows lifted from hiding behind spectacle rims, up into a forehead that had corrugated to receive them.

'Why do you say such thing?'

'You people escape the confusions bothering the rest of us?'

'Not so! We have many riots.'

'But they don't make you doubt that as a race you're quite unique.'

'This most unfair!'

'Is it? You know why you got over World War Two so quickly? You'd lost everything except a sense of being one people against the world. And that was enough to get you going again in no time at all.'

'It was *not* in no time at all, Mr Harris.'

'It was damn fast. You people are never going to be bothered by the thing that is kicking the rest of us so hard, inter-racial strife. You can't be bothered by it because your islands are peopled only by Japanese. Except a few foreigners operating under strict licence.'

'We have Koreans.'

'Mr Akamoro, if you call your Koreans a minority problem that's only because you're trying to be in fashion. You know as well as I do that Japan will never experience what is happening over beyond those trees. You can't. And you're so lucky.'

After a minute he said:

'We are not greatly loved in the world.'

'As if you cared a damn about that.'

'Oh! Not true!'

'You care about your image. You've worked hard to build that up into what you felt was required. It helps

47

sell transistors and air seats. But you don't want love from the rest of us. You have no need of it.'

'I think you speak from bitter heart, Mr Harris.'

'No. Tired sometimes. Bloody tired tonight. What is your business with me?'

His body jerked. It isn't often you trap a Japanese into showing surprise.

'Business?' That was shrill with innocence.

'Archie is easy to manipulate. You wanted a talk with me. Too private for you to ring up and ask for an appointment at my office.'

He said nothing. We walked under a huge, almost full moon which was still contriving to look placid even though it was just on the verge of being colonized by man.

'Look, Mr Akamoro, Hawakami has already given one sharp kick to my diesel engine company. Just to show me what you can do. Next step is the take-over bid, accompanied by a delicate suggestion that you'll go on kicking if I say no, and in new areas. I'm interested in your proposition. Is the idea that your subsidiary, Tatsukeshi, from now on finances my factory but keeps me on in nominal control as a front for the time and place? And as a kind of insurance against remaining local prejudice towards the Japanese?'

'You make big mistake, Mr Harris.'

'You mean you're only out here to sell tractors?'

He didn't reply.

'I'm sorry you're not getting rid of them,' I said. 'It could be another case of the need for intensive preliminary market research before the actual despatch of a selling mission.'

I was getting considerable pleasure out of being in a position to take the offensive. It was no small achievement to have discomposed a Hawakami executive.

Shouting started up again. It began as one voice, the international protest voice with a slogan, a solo aria of incomprehensible words that went on for half a minute and was then caught and swamped by the chorus. Noise suggested a sizable crowd either just beyond the park or already in it, probably moving along the road that went

48

past the gates to my house. This was going to be disturbing for Russell if he happened to have the television turned low. The widely separated mini-estates in this area were a tactical pushover if the police remained inactive and a sprawling bungalow, built entirely of timber, would make a wonderful bonfire.

Whatever Mr Akamoro was now thinking about riot noises didn't seem to worry him at all, perhaps because the residents of the world's largest city are used to violent demonstrations, Tokyo having these most week-ends. My guest for the night plodded along with his head lowered in almost total withdrawal, and I envied this gift for detachment. It's a great asset to the business executive, practically basic to success. You see the selling proposition in front of you and nothing else, and in a remarkably short time you're a senior vice-president. Mr Akamoro probably was a senior vice-president. He walked like a man who doesn't do this often, accustomed to having his weight off his legs in cars and swivel chairs and planes. He also suggested the citizen who only gets home to eat a late meal and sleep from a prescription.

The moment I heard police sirens I knew that I'd been waiting for them as the tensed up suburban dweller who has a lot to lose in any major breakdown of law and order. They were the voice of my side, of uniforms and justices of the peace, and I felt a sudden sting of shame.

Headlights flickered through the trees ahead and the tone of the shouting underwent a change. Someone started to use an amplifier and I didn't think for a moment it was a rioter. Then there were three bangs from a gun.

Mr Akamoro looked up.

'Ah,' he said.

He'd been waiting for reassurance, too.

'I've just remembered,' I said, 'that my neighbour one over is a junior cabinet minister.'

'So?'

'Trouble has to be pushed away from his door. I live on the way to it.'

If my cynicism reached the Japanese he gave no sign. After a moment he said :

49

'Tomorrow, I think, will be quiet once more.'

The note of unction didn't fit my mood. Tomorrow a lull, time for a breather and prayers of thanksgiving for the restoration of civic peace in mosques, churches and possibly Hindu temples. I couldn't see the Chinese, though, burning much hopeful joss and suddenly, in my head, I heard a high pitched Anglican voice intoning : 'Give us peace in our time, O Lord.' My reaction to that particular request has always been why just *our* time? It's more or less asking the Almighty to hold up the big explosion until we've had our fun and got tidily out of the picture with our will read in decent decorum by the family lawyer. After that all chaos can be released, it won't bother us.

We stood in deep shadow under huge trees waiting for police cars and probably an armoured jeep to make a new dictatorship safe enough for us to walk home through it.

Russell appeared to be in bed, only Taro welcomed us. After I'd had the big treatment the dog inspected our guest and so thoroughly, with distressingly audible sniffs, that I had to call him off.

'He is large,' Mr Akamoro said.

'You don't recognize the breed?'

'Excuse, please?'

'A Tosa. I got him in Tokyo.'

'Ah, so?'

'Very bright,' I said. 'As might be expected.'

'You have many Japanese connections, Mr Harris.'

I poured whisky for us both, wondering how much he knew about me. Probably a great deal. Hawakami would have prepared a dossier before they moved into that Philippines action, if they hadn't got one already filed. I had the sense of having been under surveillance, but I'm used to this.

'It's late,' I said, sitting, 'but I don't mind talking business.'

Mr Akamoro put down his glass, then stared at the back of his hands. Two of the fingers on one of them were nicotine stained. Things were not going as he had planned, but he wasn't rattled. You don't get to be vice-president if you rattle easily.

'It is true I also come to Malaysia to see you, Mr Harris.'

Superficially this looked like slamming cards down on the table but what interested me was the half pack still hidden up a sleeve of his synthetic fibre jacket. I nearly said: 'Ah, so?' It's a wonderful expression with an elastic meaning potential which can be stretched from 'Really?' to 'I'm not committing myself to anything at this stage' to an ultimate 'Go to hell'. In Tokyo you can build up a reputation as a subtle linguist by just using 'Ah, so?' at regular intervals and in assorted tones. The Japanese find this unnerving from a foreigner, at once suspecting that the user has torn quite a large hole in their national paper screen and is peeping through.

Akamoro looked at me. I'd seen him at it earlier in the evening, an inspection, what one might expect from a psychiatrist who has read the case history and is about to start on the questions.

'May I speak with frankness, Mr Harris?'

'By all means.'

'I think perhaps you do not like my country?'

'Then you're mistaken.'

'You are not anti-Japanese?'

'I'm not anti-anything. I don't classify people under national tags.'

This was perhaps not quite the truth, but it was diplomacy.

'I believe you have suffered from Japan?'

'If you mean by that my father's death in one of your camps, yes. But twice I've had my life saved by Japanese.'

I left the score taking to him. He seemed startled by my pragmatic approach. Orientals expect their relations with us to be complicated by an almost totally irrational emotionalism. They believe us to be congenitally afflicted with the kind of idealism that isn't in their genes at all, an obstacle that is often very difficult for them to negotiate. I had pushed a hurdle to one side.

He considered our relative positions for a moment and then made his decision. It wasn't exactly an on the spot decision either, his job was to confirm certain conclusions already reached in Tokyo and to act on them if he saw fit. It was a responsible role. He met it with firmness.

I hadn't noticed a particular bulge from the inside pocket of his jacket but he brought out a wallet that looked as though it was being made to do service as an attaché case, containing a great load of documents he kept close to his heart. One of these was extracted, unfolded, and passed to me.

It was a map that might have been torn from a company prospectus, of the South China Sea, and on it were dotted lines travelling north from the island of Tandjungpinang off Singapore until well up towards latitude ten, then dropping back on to Borneo near Kuching, in all enclosing an area of some five hundred square miles of possibly the world's shallowest marine waters.

'This has meaning for you, Mr Harris?'

'I wouldn't be much of a businessman out here if it didn't. This is the oil search concession area granted by Indonesia's national agency, Pertamina, to about twenty companies. All of them scrambling like mad for the really big finds they can switch to when the Middle East finally blows up.' I looked at him. 'And there are Japanese companies in on this deal?'

He nodded.

'True. But with poor hopes of great profits, I think.'

I didn't have to ask what he meant. Indonesia has come back into the world again from her period of playing footy-footy with Communism but she has done it with eyes wide open to making the best deals for herself. She has demanded, and got, from one oil company seven million dollars before that company was even allowed to begin its search, and with the guarantee of another three million dollars ex gratia payment when output reaches 50,000 barrels a day, plus the sharing of all profits on the basis of 65% to Pertamina and 35% to the company putting up finance and doing the dirty work. When I read about those terms they seemed a thoroughly unattractive proposition, but in the desperate hunt for oil not only was a taker found, but there were nineteen other takers for similar deals, including a couple of Japanese firms. A real gusher from under the seas could make these blackmail terms viable economically, but it wasn't the kind of gamble I'd go for.

I handed back the map.

'Hawakami aren't interested in this particular search area?'

'We are not, Mr Harris.'

I was now damn certain that there was some other area they *were* interested in and my pulse rate went up just slightly.

'How about a search in this country?'

That should have fused a large Chinese firecracker under his composure, but it didn't.

'There is no need.'

I tried not to stare at the man. Akamoro sat waiting quietly for me to prod him. It was more than irritating to have him playing the inscrutable Oriental, a role which doesn't fit too well on his countrymen these days, most of whom have chucked it to get on with hard selling.

'What do you mean by no need for a search?'

'We already know there is oil in Malaysia, Mr Harris.'

I lifted my glass and took a sip.

'In commercial quantities?'

'Yes.'

'If you're so sure of that Hawakami must have paid a steep price for their information. I won't ask who got the money. You wouldn't tell me.'

'I will tell you this, we did not buy. We have, you might say, inherited knowledge.'

'You've *what*?'

He was now on tricky ground. He didn't want to tell me too much, at the same time he had committed himself in a certain depth.

'I will explain. Discovery of oil is not made by my company. This made many years ago. Before World War Two.'

I couldn't help staring then.

'A Japanese company?'

He nodded.

'Are you telling me, Mr Akamoro, that your people

have been sitting on a discovery like this for more than thirty years?'

He put a cigarette in an ash-tray, then reached out to pick up his whisky in both hands, as though it was ceremonial green tea.

'There is nothing else for us to do. At that time war came quickly. When we have established Co-Prosperity in South Asia there is no need for development of new fields. We have much oil from Borneo and Java. When the war is over how can Japanese company exploit? We have no capital for many years. When this is corrected we then experience great hostility against admitting our companies into Malaysia. This situation is not yet completely cured, but perhaps no longer so serious obstacle. You must understand, until now we can do nothing.'

Except hug their secret tight and wait, as they are so good at doing.

It was plain why I was being approached. The situation demanded a go-between, someone well dug into Malaysia who was also a neutral between Chinese and Malay interests. There weren't too many candidates with these qualifications which was why they had been forced to select me. Perhaps I should have been flattered, but I wasn't. Akamoro hadn't just dropped by for a preliminary sounding out, he had come to see me armed. I was already in the spiked maiden of ruthless undercutting. All Hawakami had to do was to continue to turn the handle until blood really started to flow. And to make this quite plain they had, practically overnight, taken that Manila franchise away from me. If they really set their minds to it Harris and Company could be a corpse in a very short time indeed. I simply wasn't capitalized to fight them and they knew it.

I thought of their Kabuki drama in that big Tokyo theatre, of curtain up on an empty stage to give the audience time to appreciate how beautifully it has been set, every subtle detail considered even to the wired-on paper cherry blossoms trembling on a synthetic tree. The audience is given about three minutes to take all this in before a two sworded Samurai comes on from the wings making gargling rage noises deep in his throat.

'I think we'll have another drink,' I said.

Akamoro didn't protest. I took glasses to a side table and stood there for longer than needed to fill them.

The Japanese were thick on the ground back in the Malaysia of the thirties. They owned strategically placed rubber estates and ran trading companies with an active side line in espionage. They mapped the country in incredible detail for military use later and could easily have carried out preliminary surveys for oil without the relaxed British authority of that time getting a single clue about what they were up to. At the same time you can never be sure that there is oil until you have drilled for it and if Hawakami were so positive this could only mean that there had been drilling, real probes, possibly even a well or two brought in which had then been capped and sealed.

It isn't easy to be discreet about drilling for oil, but if their search area had been wild country, or even secondary jungle it might have been possible to conduct the final operation without attracting unwanted attention from natives or government officials. The big problem would be getting what you needed to the site and a strategically located Japanese owned rubber estate couldn't have served as supply base, strange equipment coming to it would certainly have been noticed. The cover they needed had to be something much bigger than that, an industrial complex of some kind which they owned and which was isolated enough to give them a kind of autonomy in the area of its operation.

To my knowledge there was only one such place in the country before World War Two, the iron ore mine at Dungun on the east coast of the thinly populated state of Trengganu. Japanese enterprise had opened this up and their own imported labour had run it. The ore was shipped to Japan in their own vessels, a continuous coming and going of men and material which continued until a very short time before Pearl Harbour. The area was thinly administered by the British and any unusual activity reported could have been cloaked under a Japanese claim that they were searching for further ore strata. No one would have tried to stop them doing that. In a suddenly rubber

55

rich and tin mad Malaysia no one would have been very interested.

I came back across the room and put a refilled glass in front of my guest, then sat again opposite him.

'Mr Akamoro, I have pretty good reasons for believing that your secret has leaked.'

For two seconds he looked as shocked as though I had produced a gun and pointed it at him. But recovery was quick, he even managed a smile.

'You joke, I think?'

'No. I have evidence that a big Chinese corporation is now far enough on with their search in this country to have brought in a Middle East expert for final confirmation. To me this suggests they were acting on a lead. Their hunt seems to be in jungle.'

He stared at me from behind those round glasses, but there were no signs of panic.

'There is now oil craze, Mr Harris. Not only the place I show you on map. There are now drilling rigs off Thailand, soon off Malaysia.'

'This has nothing to do with rigs. My guess is a search somewhere between the Dungun and Kelantan rivers.'

The Chinese firecracker finally exploded. Shock and fear weren't quickly covered.

'Impossible! I tell you . . .'

He stopped. He didn't have anything to tell me. He was winded. I watched him pull out a handkerchief and wipe the palms of his hand. Then he said in Japanese:

'*Kore wa taihen da*!'

I agreed with him. It was very bad news indeed for Hawakami. I decided to make it a little worse.

'You know, Mr Akamoro, I just don't see how this Chinese firm could have come by thirty-year-old information on file in your Tokyo offices. Also, I can't believe that a concern like Hawakami would take the plunge into the completely new field of oil operations without first updating that filed information. It would be fairly easy to do, if you knew exactly where you were going. Illegal entry, of course. But Malaysia has plenty of back doors, including

56

quite a number of half-forgotten landing strips in or near jungle.'

Akamoro was now sitting straight up in his chair. He was a slightly overfed businessman but for seconds I was reminded of the Samurai in Kabuki drama who sees no future with honour and is composing himself for the final *haiku* to be followed by cut belly. Then he blinked twice and was contemporary again.

'You make wild guess, Mr Harris.'

'Well, not so wild, actually. There have been great changes in Malaysia since the heyday of that Dungun mine. More people in Trengganu for one thing. For another, the Chinese corporation I'm talking about has wide interests in the country, a network of them. Their intelligence service is good. I know for a fact that they own rubber in Kelantan and they may very well control estates in Trengganu, too. They go in for a lot of proxy holding against any possible threat from monopoly laws. Their organization gives them agents on the ground almost anywhere in this country. My suggestion is that your discreet little check up team on a flying visit was spotted, reported and followed to point X. Probably its operations were watched all the time they were going on. Hence the Middle East expert snatched from his job and brought here.'

'What is the name of this Chinese company?'

'I'll tell you as soon as you point out on a map exactly where your oil is.'

'No!'

'Too soon yet in our progress towards mutual trust?'

He was angry now and not really trying to disguise this. I wasn't really worried.

'There's one factor still working for you,' I said, 'even if these people have found your oil. It's not exactly an auspicious time for any Chinese company to be making a concession deal with the Malay government. They'll claim it's to develop rubber, of course, while taking care to see that they have full mineral rights. Fortunately, I'm in a position to stop the deal by whispering one word into the right ears . . . oil. Though, of course, I'll have to know where this place is.'

Akamoro took off his glasses and polished them with a handkerchief that had been left on one knee.

'Mr Harris, I must consult with Tokyo.'

'There's a phone in your room, but isn't it a bit late now to catch anyone at the office?'

He put on his glasses again and looked at me through them.

'Mr Akamoro, whatever your dossier may say my Japanese is just not up to a fast business exchange. You people talk like typewriters these days. So there's just no point in my listening on an extension.'

He stood.

'Please show me.'

He must be very near the top indeed if he could get Hawakami brass, possibly the old man himself, out of bed at going on for midnight. Tokyo's time zone is practically ours.

He played the humble guest in the passage, bowing once or twice. I shut a door on him and then on the way back to the sitting-room paused to listen for Russell's snoring. For a man who claims he rarely sleeps he makes a lot of noise and I heard the sounds I wanted. I didn't want my partner in on any of this, he was beginning to show clear signs of that weakening of nerve which comes with age. And I had his weak heart to think of.

The whisky waiting for me was mostly water but I still didn't touch it, this was no time to risk a fuzzing. I sat down and thought about oil. It is rarely found on the slopes of mountains, and Trengganu is mountainous, the coastal strip soon rising towards the main range. Southern Kelantan seemed a more likely area. Certainly it was a long way from that old Japanese base at Dungun, but those long ago searches could have been pushed well north without too much difficulty, the only big town to be avoided Kuala Trengganu and it's not very big.

Kelantan has managed to remain reasonably isolated from the contemporary world. A dream of the tropic Orient still holds up there, little *kampongs* set back from long beaches, with palms and casuarinas, no industry, no strife, nothing really that the rest of the world wants except

58

perhaps its peace. I had thought about building a house there one day, sprawling, of wood, in the Malay style. Chicha lizards would move in with me and it would be open to breezes blowing from the South China Sea. Under lurid sunsets and glittering dawns my active past would be commented on with unbarbed irony by a people all around whose own pasts had been inactive, and happy. The place gave you this feeling, an almost totally lost feeling of a happy people.

I knew what oil would do to the State. I could already see the derricks and the pipe lines and the tin-roofed huts, with the invaders sweating under metal helmets. The people in the *kampongs* would be curious at first, then alarmed, then really frightened. They would watch the new roads being laid over their rutted tracks, and the new buildings going up, and all through tropic nights a great glare of lights from arcs. A sea terminal would be built for the tankers, a long jetty thrust out over waters so clear you could see the bright fish thirty feet down. Pollution would start, fouling the golden hems of land. There would be a takeover bid of noise. The by-product of all this would be jobs for some of the locals who hadn't wanted jobs or needed them, and electricity suddenly in the little houses to work the new refrigerators. A place which had exported a modest quota of copra via rusting coastal steamers would become a consumer market for the first time in its history and the capital of Kota Bharu would swell like a python that has just swallowed an old and not easily digested goat.

All this would be partly my doing, but if I opted out someone else would take over. It's always the answer. The consortium I had in mind would be Malay slanted which was better than seeing Min Kow Lin laughing and getting richer. We needed capital from somewhere and suddenly Hawakami were offering unlimited yen on a platter.

I thought about what I knew of an old man at the head of a huge complex based on Tokyo. He had been purged by MacArthur, of course, as one of the *Zaibatsu* industrialists who weren't to be allowed a role at all in the new Japan. Hawakami had retired to a country villa for six months before starting to work again through proxies. By nineteen fifty-two he was back in his old seat controlling coal, engineering, ship-building and fifty million cans of fish per annum. A few years later he was making marine diesels as a side line and about that time hit on the interesting new democratic idea of morning prayer meetings in all his factories to keep up worker morale. Someone wrote a company hymn which the thousands of Hawakami employees were obliged to sing before they settled at work benches. And their declaration of faith wasn't beamed towards a god they couldn't see. The Emperor of Japan may have publicly renounced his divinity a quarter of a century ago but the *Zaibatsu* never demoted themselves in this drastic way, they just stepped back into the shadows to wait for their time to come again, which it had soon enough.

It seemed to me likely that Akamoro was at the moment phoning the boss himself. I was pretty certain he was big enough to share the platform with Hawakami on those occasions when the company head made personal appearances at the morning ceremonies, and probably with a seat close in to the central one occupied by a bright-eyed old man.

My guest for the night stood in the doorway, looking grave but in no way discomposed, as though he had just received authorization to proceed against the unforeseen as he saw fit. He bowed, lower than he had been doing. The gesture was much more than routine politeness, it signified change in the relation between us. I was to be accorded full honours as a colleague, the status to be generally recognized right up to that moment when they decided, regretfully, that my head was for the chopper.

CHAPTER IV

Mr Akamoro bent over a half-inch to the mile Ordnance map of northern Malaysia, with propelling pencil poised while he got his bearings. Then he stabbed down and

60

made a circle on the paper, quite a large circle. The map at once became a top secret document for my office safe. The oil field was in southern Kelantan, not far from the border with Trengganu.

He looked at me.

'The Chinese company, Mr Harris?'

'Min Kow Lin.'

'Ah, so?'

That was let out on a long hiss. What he knew about Min he didn't like. Neither did I.

'I'll get my assistant up to this area at once for a snoop.'

'And if he discovers geologist in Kelantan?'

'There's no need for panic stations. Isn't this a rubber estate inside your circle.'

'Yes. Just on the edge, near the sea. It is only fringe of oil area, but still important, I think.'

It was important all right.

'Who owns it?'

'Chinese independent.'

'You're sure? I told you Min has a lot of proxies.'

'We check most carefully. The estate is poorly run. Very small value, I think. Impossible that Min already own this place.'

'Well they'll be out to buy it now, I can tell you. We've got to get it first.'

'Yes.'

'What about our main area? It looks like secondary jungle?'

'Totally undeveloped, Mr Harris. No village, nothing.'

That was all right. It was improbable that Min had already started to negotiate for a concession of the area, but if they had I was pretty sure I could arrange to have the matter tangled in much red tape.

'I'll start proceedings right away to form a new company called Kelantan Developments,' I said. 'With a share capital of five thousand Malay dollars subscribed by me.'

Under this arrangement Hawakami would be putting themselves entirely in my hands for the time being and Akamoro wasn't happy about this. But he had the check

61

of being able to ruin me later if I cheated and this kept him calm enough.

'And then, Mr Harris?'

'I find some directors for the board. One of them can be my partner Mr Menzies. Another must be a Malay.'

'You have a man in mind?'

'Batim Salong.'

His face said that prince's reputation was not unknown to him.

'I do not understand such a choice?'

'His Excellency the Tunku is a cousin of practically all the men who matter in the running of this country. He has royal blood. He's intelligent, but lazy. I think I can wake him up.'

Akamoro shook his head.

'The choice is not acceptable.'

'Now look, we'll get nowhere at all without a Malay who counts and you know it! I happen to have an in with Batim, I don't with anyone else with his potential of usefulness. Without him I don't play. Which leaves you free to report your find to the government in the hope that they'll give you the concession. In my opinion you wouldn't get it. For one thing you'd have a number of very awkward questions to answer.'

There was a very long silence before Akamoro said:

'It would seem that I must trust your judgment.'

He hated having to do that.

By two-thirty am we had worked out a great many more details and without recourse to the whisky bottle. I poured him a night cap and took my glass to the french windows, opening them. The city seemed quiet enough, no police sirens, and no red that wasn't from neon. I shut the window again and turned.

'We haven't discussed my price, Mr Akamoro. What does Tokyo think that is?'

The blunt question could have damaged an emerging relationship with a lot of people, but not my guest. He might have been waiting to tell me.

'After initial formation of company we meet all further expenses. You will receive retaining fee. This will be two hundred and fifty thousand US dollars paid into Swiss bank.'

I felt I was worth a lot more.

'I don't have a Swiss bank.'

'This easily arranged at any time through Tokyo. There will also be further payment to you of the same amount when Kelantan Developments come fully under control of my company.'

I got half a million greenbacks for all my work and a scheduled fade out at the end of it.

'What about my co-directors?'

'We will arrange suitable fees for them, also.'

I sat down again. Akamoro did the talking. He might have been reading from a Tokyo briefing, everything thought out, no loose ends. I stayed on the board of Kelantan Developments until the oil really started to flow, all the way as a front man. The real business would be done by a general manager experienced in oil who was to be lured from his present job by bright new prospects but not given a seat on the board. Akamoro estimated that the field ought to be in full production within two years. When this stage had been reached first one Hawakami man and then a second would be quietly infiltrated as new directors. This would leave the original directors in apparent control, three to one, but quite suddenly Russell, feeling the weight of his years, would accept a golden handshake and resign. I would do the same on the grounds of pressure from my other businesses. This would leave Malay interests continuing to be represented by the man I had demanded, but Tokyo in control.

Hawakami were running a risk, of course, and knew it. There was a chance that I might decide I liked the oil business and not want to leave it. In the event of my causing trouble of this kind I would forfeit that second two hundred and fifty thousand as well as earning the undying enmity of Hawakami enterprises which would be most unhealthy for Harris and Company. Also, and this

63

was ingenious, I wasn't going to be paid a salary from Japan, just those two additions to capital, one now, one when I retired gracefully.

'The Japanese are going to win the peace,' I said.

Mr Akamoro stayed solemn.

'To allies we are just and fair.'

'I'm sure of that. There's a little matter of diesel engines. A franchise in Manila I'd very much like to get back. You know what I'm talking about?'

'Yes.'

'Well?'

'Price cutting now over,' he said.

We breakfasted on the verandah. I had the impression that Akamoro was suffering from a slight hangover, though he was looking remarkably tidy in an uncrushable suit and freshly drip-dried shirt. These days the traveller with no luggage at all can stay neat. As the debris of our technology increasingly threatens to swamp us we keep our persons immaculate.

After half an hour of minimal talk, none of it drifting in the direction of business, we were joined by my partner. I took one look at him and knew at once that this morning he was switched off and meant to stay that way. When Russell is switched on . . . he likes to set his own times for this . . . his charm can be almost overwhelming, particularly to people newly exposed to it, and guests leave us at the end of an on session with an awareness of having just experienced one of life's really important things, stimulated by an old man's wit and warmed by his basic humanity.

Now he was operating on minimal revs., just ticking over. He had put on a bathrobe after a shower, tying this shut with a couple of tasselled cords, but not very effectively. He was wearing nothing underneath and sat down looking like the leading baritone in a new musical who is just about to add a note of rough realism to the big nude scene, meantime wrapped in towelling because of a draught from the wings. He hadn't shaved.

Akamoro had done his homework and knew a good deal

about Russell, possibly more than I did, and there hadn't been a hint of any opposition to my partner on the board of Kelantan Developments. It was pretty obvious, though, that the Japanese was now having a hard time fitting the dossier to the man. And Russell didn't help at all. He accepted the introductions with a nod, and a cup of coffee without one, then sat looking like a Hogarth drawing of what a life of sin does for you in the end. The only contribution he offered towards the entertainment of a guest was to flex fingers on two plump, mottled hands, letting early sun get at his arthritis.

It suddenly occurred to me that those snores could have been artificial and last night Russell had, in fact, crept down a corridor to listen to talk in the sitting-room. If he'd done that there was a big storm brewing for when we were alone.

The sound of a car coming up the drive at that hour was something of a surprise, it was too early for the vans and the post had been, and I was positively startled by the sign on the roof which said: 'Police. Stop!' Akamoro rose.

'Mr Harris, in my room I have taken liberty of phoning to police station. I ask for car to take me to hotel. I think this is best policy. Please accept deep thanks for kind hospitality. And Mr Menzies, it is great pleasure to meet you.'

'Oh, yes,' Russell said, committing himself to nothing.

We watched Akamoro go, straight down the steps, since he had nothing to carry except that wallet. A sergeant got out of the front of the car and opened a back door. Akamoro had charming old world Nipponese courtesy for the representative of law and order. He wasn't one of the new breed of his country's go-getters who have learned in commercial school all about the brisk, firm handshake and using first names from round one. I hadn't been told to call him Ken, short for Kenichi.

The car moved.

'What the hell was all that about?' Russell asked.

'He was at the Potters'. The idea of a police car to take him to his hotel didn't seem a good thing last night, they were all busy. I offered him a bed.'

'And just who is he?'

'A tractor salesman.'

'What company?'

'Obori Agricultural Machinery.'

'That's a Hawakami subsidiary.'

I didn't deny it.

'Big hearted of you to entertain one of them, after Manila.'

'I forgive easily.'

Russell stirred in his chair.

'You didn't think of calling me last night to help with the entertaining?'

I could feel the beam of suspicion from six feet away.

'Well, I thought about it. But you were snoring. And with your sleep problem it seemed a shame to disturb you.'

'Voices woke me. At two!'

'We were discussing Zen Buddhism. It got quite animated. Mr Akamoro goes into regular retreat at a monastery. It helps his business drive. I'm thinking of trying it. He's offered to give me an introduction to a temple in the Izu peninsula that takes paying guests.'

'Did that man come here with an offer from Hawakami? A take-over offer for your diesels?'

'No.'

'You're up to something, Paul.'

'You brood too much.'

The phone rang. I went into the house and picked up the receiver.

'This is Jean Hyde.'

'Hello. No trouble your way, I hope?'

'We're serene. I believe there's been some sort of vigilante squad of the local men patrolling the street, but I haven't seen it. My worry is personal. All the other men I've met in riots have tried to date me next day. Why didn't you?'

'I'm a great respecter of husbands.'

'I said you were a period piece. Would a lunch be too dangerous?'

'Not if we avoid a private room. Today?'

'I'm free. But make it somewhere quiet.'

66

'Under martial law the club ought to be pretty quiet. It'll take a few days to get back to norm.'

'I don't think I want to be exposed to sahibs.'

'The species is almost extinct. I'll meet you there at one.'

'Oh . . . all right.'

'Any contact with your husband?'

'Yes. He rang me last night.'

'Where from?'

'You know, I didn't ask. He'd come into some town, though, but only for an hour or so. I told him not to worry about me. Knowing John, he won't.'

The Geological Department is housed in the half-cellar of a new block built for the Ministry of Agriculture and Forestry. If I had been Hugh Gilston I'd have rejected those offices, but he isn't the rejecting type, a half-scientist, half-civil-servant who has voted for no punch ups in his world, a man who has slipped easily into the round hole provided. I play golf with him sometimes because he is slightly worse than I am.

Hugh's desk was a clutter with coffee pot and used cup still left on it. He was bent so far forward over some work I could see his bald spot. He didn't look up.

'Yes?'

'Sorry to bother you.'

'Good God, Paul! What brings you slumming?'

'I want a look at your survey files.'

'Of course. Geological surveys?'

'That's it.'

'I'm not supposed to ask of what area?'

He smiled. It made him look much younger.

'I'd prefer just to be led to your shelving and left. Unless that's against regulations. Is there a security factor?'

'Officially. In fact, no. You're welcome to all of it. And the dust.'

We went into the cement floored passage I had used to get to his office. It was a tunnel from the back of the building to the front with a glazed door at each end to hold in the air conditioning. Rows of labelled wooden doors opened off it to one side but there were none at all along the other until we came to a steel panel fitted with a mortice lock. Hugh came into the file-room with me, offering more explanations than I needed about how a fairly primitive indexing system worked. The place had three deep bays formed by racks of open shelving that went up to eight feet and needed a portable ladder to reach the top layers. Cardboard holders filled most of the space though there were some gaps.

'No need to lock you in,' Hugh said. 'Will you be some time?'

'Probably.'

'I lunch early. If I should be away to the canteen just put the key on my desk, will you?'

Nothing was said about our riots. In official circles these were being played down. The door clanged. It was a little like being in a jail, concrete underfoot and up the walls, everything else, except for the files, metal, including a desk and a chair.

Complete computerization is going to bring its problems for me. I stood in a repository for perhaps eighty years of the life work of local geologists, most of them now as dead as their reports, realizing that if all this information had been stored in an electronic brain bank I simply couldn't have asked a friend for the key and then browsed for what I wanted. Machines don't tolerate the casual approach, you have to declare your requirements to the highly trained technician who punches out a card for your ration of facts. An element of secrecy, important at the moment, just wouldn't be possible.

I got interested in my files. Two characters had been slightly concerned with the area in which I was concentrating, one clearly young from a tendency to unscientific digressions which he hadn't quite learned to eliminate, the other obviously a departmental head who every now and then made the definitive field trip to clear up any uncertainties left by junior assistants. The old boy made a great act of being sure of himself, but this couldn't cover the fact that his conclusions were theoretical and mostly guesswork. It didn't take me too long to find out that even the accessible areas of southern Kelantan had not been surveyed in any depth by government geologists, the job left to the unauthorized back in the 1930's who had failed to submit a copy of their report for official records.

I didn't think that Min Kow Lin had originally been led to Kelantan oil by anything recorded here but it still seemed possible that something in these files might have suggested the State as an area to watch. In fact there was nothing like that, not even a discussion of the chances of oil strata being found, the whole fixation being on tin. This indicated one thing pretty closely, that Min's intelligence organization was even better than I had thought it was. The chances were that they were in a position to know about any unusual activity almost anywhere in the country while local police and officialdom suspected nothing. Routine industrial espionage didn't begin to account for such an elaborate set-up, it suggested something very near to a secret society apparatus that would certainly serve the Corporation's commercial activities but could also do a lot more than that. It might even indicate that Min were poised to take a hand in political activity the moment the right opportunity presented itself and I knew well what beam that would be on, Malaysia for the Chinese. I was suddenly slightly less anti the recent establishment of martial law than I had been.

The Chinese may give lip service to multi-racial societies but they don't really believe in them, only Chinese societies. Where they are able to they take power, where they can't as yet they wait, and this isn't a political and social philosophy which leaves a great deal of room for treating other races on terms of equality.

There was a footnote to the report in front of me that I hadn't followed up, it referred to another file. The index directed me to the central bay which I hadn't yet visited and I went around the end of shelving. The new aisle was exactly like the one I had left, with a desk and table at the far end. There was also another man engaged on research, looking for something on a low shelf, squatting with his face away from me in maximum available shadow.

Hugh was responsible for these archives and whatever

he might say about their importance they had a certain value. I was fairly sure that he kept the only key in use and that no one, even perhaps his own office staff, came in here without his authorization. Certainly the key had been left unturned in the lock and it was just possible that someone who knew I was using the place had decided to pop in for a moment to check something. But this man must have come in very quietly indeed. Concrete and steel amplify sound but all the time I'd been reading I'd heard absolutely nothing, not even the sound of feet in the corridor beyond.

'You work in the department?' I asked politely.

The man straightened. He had good leg muscles, shooting up smoothly like a gymnast. Light from high windows was behind him, but I could still see that he was Chinese, tall for the race. His build, too, wasn't southern, too solid, suggesting a Manchurian. There was a bulge in the right-hand pocket of his tropic weight brown jacket. He stared at me but said nothing. I changed my tone.

'Have you any right to be in here?'

There was no answer. What reached me was total hostility, a small psychic wave of this. He stood there assessing my exact position on his way to the door.

I thought I was ready for that charge. Malay boxing is a useful surprise factor when it's the last thing your opponent expects, but I had used it often enough for my little skill to be recorded in dossiers. He came hunched down, apparently the perfect target for the quick flip up of my right leg. I made contact, but not where I'd meant to. Thigh impact was useless. It served him, though. He caught my ankle and jerked up my leg. I went down on concrete.

I wasn't winded. I grabbed his foot as he went by. He tried to put his other foot in my face but the manoeuvre required a flair for ballet balance he hadn't quite got. He came down, clutching at files which failed as a handhold and toppled with him, half a row of them. Hardback covers impeded his bids to kick in my teeth with a free foot. I was still holding the other. He broke this by a

70

kind of jack-knife of his body up from the floor, and was on his feet while I was still on my knees, an offering in apparent helplessness which he couldn't resist. He came at me for a neck chop. My head went in below his rib cage hard. The chop got my right shoulder. Even there it felt like a hot flat-iron dropped from a height.

He was back against shelving, this time managing a hold. His bids to get his breath back sounded like sucking noises from a washing machine that has lost its water. I wasn't any more gentlemanly about my advantage than he would have been. I stood and put a left into his stomach to keep those noises going, then tried a follow through with a right to his jaw. The pain in my shoulder screamed. I didn't land any sledge hammer blow, but apparently it was enough. He began to droop down in front of steel shelves as though his legs were telescoping stilts.

The man's descent would have looked fine in a Western. He managed to keep his back against an upright even while his knees buckled then gave up and toppled forward, looking as though he was going to fall on his face. This didn't happen, he did a half-turn and landed on his back, arms stretched out. Under one of his wrists was the jagged scar of a knife wound so deep it was a miracle he had recovered the full use of that hand.

His eyes were shut. I went for the bulge in a jacket pocket. It wasn't a gun, just a miniaturized pair of field glasses, Japanese manufacture, 7 x 35, handy for bird watching or reading small print at a distance.

I made the mistake of looking at them for too long. The glasses went off on a flight of their own as two feet landed in my stomach, the soles of his shoes wired to springs just released. I went half-way down the aisle in a semi-erect posture but finished the distance in a slide on my bottom. The desk held me up. It was my turn for the washing-machine noises.

He got up, standing to look at me, wanting to really finish it. Every natural instinct he possessed was urging that he do this, but apparently a higher discipline was still functioning. He turned and walked towards the door.

Whooping as I certainly was I still had the satisfaction of seeing that he was far from upright, hunched in pain. The metal door closed quietly.

I went into the men's washroom at the club feeling pretty sure I was going to be sick. My body felt as though I had just lived through a half hour session with a near homicidal masseur. There were aches where there was no real reason for these to be at all and a red throbbing from the places entitled to them.

I had a look at my face. It hadn't been marked up in any way, all it said was that I had passed my best years for a rough house. I washed, and combed my hair, trying to control pain twitches.

It was a bit of a surprise to find the club humming, as though half its membership had decided to celebrate an ending of the troubles even before this was officially announced. Wives were out in force, too, their voices particularly marked from the verandah bar. I went into it and got greeting signals from a number of tables, as though I was a popular chap in my own right instead of just the man who was always there at Russell's parties. Most of the stools up at the bar counter were taken and on two of them, side by side, were Archie Potter and Mr Akamoro. I joined them. I didn't think it was policy to avoid contact with my recent guest though from the look on his face he had been half-expecting this.

'What are you having?' Archie asked.

'A double whisky neat and I'll buy it.'

I bought their second round, too.

'Everyone's here today,' Archie told us.

'Peace now returns,' Akamoro announced, as though he had just concluded a successful mission for UNO.

It was pretty obvious that Archie had been making heavy weather with the man from Japan towards whom he had a certain responsibility and he was quick at producing a poorly dressed excuse to leave us. The bellowing round about provided a high degree of privacy.

'There is a tail on me,' I said.

'Excuse, please?'

'I've just had a set to with a character who could be on Min's payroll.'

'Set to?'

'Fight.'

Akamoro was shocked.

'Is this possible?'

'It happened and I've got the marks to prove it. He was a pro. A knife man, too. Though he didn't seem to be carrying one this morning.'

'*Ah, yoku nai, na!*'

'We're in a *yoku nai* business now, Mr Akamoro.'

'What will you do?'

'Stick to my plans. See Batim Salong. If I land the prince I'll get up to Kelantan and start negotiating to buy that rubber estate.'

'Where are you attacked?'

'In a file-room. He wanted out in a hurry. I tried to stop him, but didn't succeed. The man's equipment included glasses to spy on what I was researching. That was Kelantan surveys. From now on we're operating with Min on our tail. They'll be on to you, too. They know where you were last night and that you're from Hawakami.'

Akamoro looked most unhappy.

'This place . . . safe for talking?'

'Yes, provided you keep a social smile on your face. Second safest place in Kuala Lumpur. The club's integrated, but do you see any Chinese?'

I thought he might have a quick look around but he didn't, he was wearing the social smile and spoke through visible teeth.

'Where is most safe place in this city?'

'Oddly enough a Chinese restaurant. They've built up their business on food and security. Both are tops. It's called Yung Ching Wa's. We're meeting there tomorrow night at seven-thirty. There'll be a room booked. And we don't have to worry about bugging.'

The bar was now really seething, with the din reaching cocktail party decibels. I asked Akamoro if he was lunching with Archie but he wasn't.

'Then I suggest you go back to your hotel,' I said. 'By

taxi. Stay there until tomorrow night. Don't go out to do any sightseeing and don't make long distance calls to Tokyo, even in code.'

He had a lot of questions but I gave him full marks for not asking them. He left the bar as though he was looking for the men's room and I was pretty sure that Archie, now with a party at one of the tables, didn't notice. A moment or two later I went out into the foyer myself but could see no sign of the Japanese. I lit a cigar and left air-conditioning for the heat of the courtyard. Across from the club one of the small patches of jungle which still survive in the city was steaming away damp from a sudden morning shower.

I didn't recognize the woman who got out of the taxi, not even when she looked at me. It was probably her hat, which was black, of some kind of floppy material with an enormous brim that hid her eyes. That headpiece looked straight out of a late night movie originally screened back in 1932 when talking pictures were still something of an innovation. The dress went with it, in midi length of which I hadn't seen too much, an extraordinary print of large black flowers on a white background.

The girl looked like a royal widow just permitted, after six months, to make the first tentative moves away from official court mourning. Her blonde hair had all been tucked away up under that hat and this left her face positively skeletal in boning. She moved as though her body was trying to reject all that curtain material for a back bedroom, wanting into slacks and a shirt again. I hadn't seen such a red lipstick for years and it was the kind that keeps a wet look.

'Sorry I'm late,' Jean Hyde said.

I was thinking about our quiet little lunch and whether or not I could sneak her straight into the dining-room, but I had the feeling she wouldn't like that, it would spoil her act. She had put on all this fancy dress not because it was the latest thing from the boutiques but for the squares she expected to find occupying this place. This was all a big nose thumb from the seventies back towards an era for which there is now both nostalgia and contempt, the Noel

74

Coward music, and imperial flags still waving above native gardeners sweating while they clipped lawn edges. As we went into the verandah bar she said in a voice that carried well in spite of the row:

'What's it like on a busy day?'

Club lunches are not really very dressy affairs and most of the women were still in last year's as-near-as-they-had-dared minis, which meant exposed thighs out on to the verandah and not one of them were topped off with a hat. Mrs Jean Hyde got the deep tribute of an almost immediate silence started by her sex but supported by the men, who were staring. It became so quiet that the rustle of that long skirt was distinctly audible.

A man got off his stool and offered it. This seemed less a gracious act than a desire to be somewhere else before his wife's best friend spotted him in strange company. A moment later I got a stool, too. The barman was attentive, which had nothing to do with my rating in the place. Jean tucked up square toed shoes on a cross bar showing about as much ankle as a Victorian nanny, then said:

'Well, this is certainly something to see. Once.'

'What will you have?'

She thought this over.

'What about a Singapore gin sling? Isn't that the right thing?'

The barman was an old hand but I don't think he had been asked to make one of those for twenty years. Quite a few of the other customers watched fascinated while he did it.

'Who's allowed in here?' Jean Hyde asked still in that voice which travelled.

'Anyone with the cover charge.'

'So if I got a temporary membership I could bring in my cab driver?'

'I don't see why not.'

'A lot of others round here would, though. How long do you think you can make it last?'

'What?'

'Pretending that the white man didn't have the hell kicked out of him in these parts about the time I was born.'

'We don't pretend anything.'

'No? Take a look at the cars in the parking lot. Or the standard home pattern. It's like Daddy's dream of the good days. Two house servants and two outside. And the cook boy still does the shopping and cheats in his accounts and everyone knows it but what does it matter anyway because all he gets is a sweated wage.'

'You ought to have brought a banner,' I said. 'And it's easily seen you haven't paid a servants' bill since you arrived. Min Kow Lin pick up the tab for you, do they?'

Under the droop of that brim her remarkable eyes widened.

'Why, you snooping bastard,' she said.

She didn't much like the taste of her drink. I bought a pack of King size and gave her a cigarette. In the flare of the match she looked straight into my eyes, her face set. I wondered what John Hyde was like and whether, in spite of what she had said about him, the wife was chairman of their combine. It was hard to see this girl giving love. She would give plenty of sex if the inducements were right.

We had the privacy of bar noise again.

'Have the Hydes got any roots?' I asked.

'No. Should we?'

'I have. Here.'

She smiled.

'The loot's super, like I said.'

'I could have done a lot better with my original stake somewhere else.'

'What keeps you here, then? An easy change over in Chinese girl-friends?'

'I like the place.'

'Really? Your experience of the rest of the world must be limited.'

'I don't want to see Malaysia become part of the shambles that's happening to the north of us.'

'By which you mean a Chinese takeover? I don't know the first thing about Far East politics and I don't want to. John and I move from one mess to another. That's all there is these days. Whenever you're going somewhere new count on it being a mess and you'll be okay.'

76

'With no hope?'

'What's hope? The kind of thing my Daddy believes in? The happy days back again of people touching their caps to the bosses. That's finished. Wiped out.'

'Who takes over? Communists?'

'Of course not. Pirates. All effective businesses these days fly the black flag. I thought you did, too?'

I drank my whisky.

'What about the idealism of the contemporary young?'

'What about it? They're just kids who haven't had their first taste of the sweet things.'

'Where do you stack your loot?' I asked.

'Switzerland. Where else? It's in every contract John signs. We keep three rooms in Beirut as our base, which makes it easy.'

'You escape taxes?'

'Practically. In South America we had to make the gesture, we didn't really get on to the corruption pattern until we were leaving. But in the Middle East the oil companies handle everything for you, even with their short contract men. It's smooth and sweet.'

John Hyde's short contracts would be for fat fees.

'What happens when your husband decides he's worked enough? Settle in Beirut?'

'Hell, no! It's a sink. We live on a boat, paying harbour dues, nothing else. Maybe the Greek islands. John likes the Carribean but the way things are happening over there I'd always have the feeling we weren't going to have time to clear harbour away from one of the local explosions.'

This girl would probably be John Hyde's widow one day, but I couldn't see her as his ex-wife. Their intricate financial arrangements practically ruled out divorce. It's one way of achieving marital stability.

I didn't think that John Hyde had come to Malaysia on salary, even a very good salary. They had left the Middle East in a hurry, almost certainly with a broken contract behind them, which meant a real inducement. Hyde must have seen a considerable number of his explorations resulting in really big money to the people employing him while he got a bonus cheque and a see-you handshake.

If I'd been in the survey business I'd soon begin to want more than my free-lance fee, taking a cue from the big name film actors who only function on a percentage of the take. Could Min have offered him that? Why not? Hyde would be useful to them for a lot more than just a confirmation of that Kelantan find. With his contacts in the oil business all over the world he could help them build up their exploitation team, and that way would be worth a small percentage on future barrel production. A well goes on giving for a long time. If this deal went all right for Min the Hydes could be on their tax-evading boat in a couple of years.

From under that hat the girl was looking around the room, at what she labelled the sahibs but dismissed as petty traders, not pirates, most of whom would end up on pensions with tight budgets and wondering how they were going to meet inflation. Even the cosy England of their dream schedules was growing less cosy every year while they sweated it out in the tropics. They had Jean Hyde's contempt. Perhaps for different reasons I had it too, and this galled me. One thing was certain, I didn't make her in the least nervous. It had taken her about ten seconds to recover from the slight shock of realizing that I knew her husband was working for Min. She had lived the kind of life which gave her a high immunity reaction to sudden unpleasant surprises.

'Let's eat,' I said.

'All right. What's the food like?'

'Rather British.'

She screwed up her face.

That lunch confirmed that John Hyde was an oil geologist and nothing but an oil geologist. The girl worked fairly hard to convince me that this was not the case, oil a sort of side line for her husband, his real interest tin, which he had hunted for in Chile before their brief session in the Middle East. I didn't believe her for one minute, there's oil in Chile, too. She saw that her tactic wasn't getting across but this didn't seem to make her nervous, though about all she had for nourishment was cigarette smoke.

On the steps outside she looked around.

'What's your second car? A Rolls?'

'Mini.'

'Are you going to drive me home?'

'Do you think you could get that hat into it?'

She turned her head to me.

'You don't sell charm, do you? For all you know I might be offering you siesta hour at my place.'

'I've got to get to the office.'

We walked to the car park. She looked at my little box.

'Is this hotted up?'

'No.'

'The Mini-Coopers are all right. We'll have one on our boat. With a derrick to lift it out.'

The Hydes weren't planning to live on a cabin cruiser, probably a hydrofoil like the one in the Bond film that could shed its outer hull and take to the air. We got into the little car and almost at once I was conscious of her watching the way I drove, so I performed like a nervous suburbanite who is thinking of giving it all up and using public transport.

'You prefer automatic?' she asked, when we were in Batu Road.

'Yes.'

She didn't say that no gears was for old men, just lit another cigarette from the pack with a warning on it. I did an appalling pass from behind a lorry that left us totally blind, accelerating jerkily straight towards an oncoming car which blared at us. Jean Hyde stopped trying to use her lighter in order to hold on, then swore softly under her breath.

I noticed that she was referring to the wing mirror on her side, unable to pick up any reason for this until we had passed two intersections and were heading east. Then I placed a following car, two back in the traffic lane. It was a Citroen Safari, with oil suspension for the kind of cornering that gets you round fast if you don't mind a touch of seasickness. I took a left turn.

'This isn't the way!' Jean said.

'I know.'

'What the hell are you doing?'

'Taking you sightseeing.'

'No, look . . .'

'Shut up and hold on.'

'*What?*'

We went down between shops. I just got around a bus that was going to hold up the Citroen, doing the kind of jerk in to make it that put a strain on my seat belt. Jean Hyde hadn't fastened hers and was flung about like one of those dummies used to test what happens to a body in a pile-up.

The city has a de-controlled four-laner that is meant for use as a by-pass and I reached this at sixty, circling a round-about and then letting the needle jerk up. At seventy-four, and somewhat oppressive wheel noise through my open window, I looked back for the Citroen to see it coming down the clear at about eighty. I pressed my foot down. We passed factories and one of the new housing estates that wasn't going up fast enough to deal with a population increase. It seemed to be all washing hanging from balconies. Then we slammed into its shopping precinct and I braked, hard. Jean went forward towards the windscreen.

She stayed hunched over, apparently needing to hold on to the parcels tray and practically hidden by that hat. When slim fingers started a sneak journey towards the ignition key I brought the heel of my left hand down on a slim wrist. She howled and jerked back.

'Min certainly uses active bait,' I said.

'You've gone mad!'

'I don't think so. There's a snatch scheduled. And you're not the target.'

There was a new supermarket in poured concrete three stories high with a service lane beside it and the backside of a huge van projecting out a foot or two on to pavement. I did a quick assessment and decided that there was just room for the Mini between the van and a brick wall. There was a space clear of pedestrians on the sidewalk. I braked into a turn that did something to my brain inside its container and seemed really to shake the girl, for she moaned. I was gambling on the lane doing a U and coming down again beyond the building. If it didn't we'd both have to take to our feet. The area behind the market seemed entirely devoted to huge iron rubbish-bins and I had to steer an obstacle course amongst these, past an open service door and a sound of canned music. I stopped the Mini, reached across the girl, and opened her door.

'Get out!'

'No!'

I gave her a shove, and it wasn't gentle. She must have caught a foot in that long skirt, one of the new hazards, for she crashed into a bin. Its lid slid off, taking a black hat to asphalt with it. Her hair streamed back into place around her shoulders. She screamed. It could have been from pain.

In the mirror I saw a man coming round the corner of the building, then a second man. Both were wearing two-piece business suits, but they didn't look like commercial travellers. I slammed the door shut, scraped a dustbin, and swung into the down lane, half-expecting to see the long shape of a Citroen blocking it, but they hadn't thought that far ahead. I bounced out into thin traffic on the wide road and went east towards the city centre, passing a parked Citroen facing the other way which didn't have a driver sitting behind the wheel. The reserves had been called out, probably to catch me as I ran through the supermarket. I hoped they would give a poor girl a lift home.

CHAPTER V

I MET His Excellency the Tunku Batim Salong years ago on the night train from Singapore to Kuala Lumpur. This was called an express but you could make the distance by car in half the time and even in those days the comfortable little air-conditioned coaches were beginning to give the feel of something outmoded and under sentence. I used rail sometimes when not in a hurry because I liked it. That journey through tropic dark with jungle reaching to the track where wilderness hadn't been cleared for oil

81

palm or rubber was time out from pressures. Lying on a berth with the window blind up I got the feeling I never had driving, that I was travelling through the land which was more mine than any other, and at a speed that allowed the feel and sounds of it to reach me. Once, during an unscheduled jungle stop, I had heard the noise a Johore tiger makes when its kill is threatened.

My feeling is for little countries not heavily populated, Malaysia, Scotland, one hot, one cold, both rough packages of mountains held by sea, and both starred by legends of human living so old that detail has been lost and only the themes remain. In Malaysia these themes are of Hindu invasions along the western coasts and to the east hints of small forgotten states that perhaps paid tribute to Han China.

Batim Salong was from the West, and though a Moslem, showed a Hindu strain in distant raja ancestry, a Malay all right, but with thinner features and a sharper profile.

There had been a commotion on the platform before we left Singapore and I'd looked out to see a crowd all in Malay dress apparently taking formal farewells of someone in my coach. As we rattled over the causeway I made for the bar car, passing the prince's door just as it opened. It was the only time I've seen him in semi-state dress, turbaned and with a jewel-handled curved knife thrust through a sash belt. He gave me a look that failed to acknowledge my presence, then went down the train, with me following.

In a canvas join up between carriages a jerk suddenly flung him back and he only managed one hand hold, his right arm smacking back into my chest. I caught hold of it. Even with the jolting I felt his body stiffen, as though physical contact with a European repelled him. But he did manage a nod and a half smile before moving on.

In the bar car we sat with a couple of empty chairs between us, the prince getting most of the service. He was drinking orange juice and eventually I got a whisky. His eyes fixed on my glass. I'd seen that look before. If the man wasn't an alcoholic he was on the road, and suffered the tortures of the deprived. There was nothing a defender of the Koran could do about this in public, either, particularly with a Malay service staff. But he had the cunning of desperation; he took out a wallet, produced a card and sent it over to me, by the waiter. I handed over my card which was put on a tray and taken back to His Excellency. We then exchanged smiles and after a moment the prince said that the train journey was a slow one and he wished that he had used his car. There wasn't much else. He finished his orange juice and left. I took longer over my drink, in fact had another.

The door to Batim Salong's compartment was open as I passed it. He was sitting still fully dressed on the berth and staring out into the corridor. The moment he saw me he said:

'Mr Harris, in the name of Allah and Dr Freud, do me a great service.'

'I'd be delighted to, Your Excellency.'

'Go to your cell and ring for the attendant. Order a bottle of whisky and then join me here for a nightcap.'

'There's no need to ring the bell. I have a flask.'

I went and found this, picked up a tooth glass and joined the prince for an informal audience.

'Shut the door,' he said.

He asked me to pour and I made it a generous medicinal dose.

'Water?'

'No.'

He took the drink with a steady hand, looked at it for a moment, then emptied the glass.

'Ah . . . thank God! For two days I've been at a family wedding. I daren't take even a half bottle with me. I have an aunt who searches cupboards. The strict piety of old Moslem women is beyond belief when you consider how little our religion does for them as a sex. Mr Harris, have you ever experienced two days of feasting without a drop of alcohol to help sustain you?'

'I've never been on a two-day feast, Your Excellency.'

'It's unspeakable. Really unspeakable.'

We didn't talk for long that night, the prince not in a mood for chat. I left the flask. It wasn't returned to me and we didn't meet in the morning at Kuala Lumpur station, but a week later a replacement was delivered by hand to the flat I then had in Singapore, Kelantan silver, delicately and intricately worked, and with it an invitation to dinner the next time I was up country.

In his house just north of Seremban the Tunku spends a lot of his life in bed. This is quite a bed, too, one that might have been designed for the wedding night of a Hapsburg except that there are no gilded nudes, just a carved, formalized leaf motif keeping decoration within the Mohammedan tradition. The headboard goes up for all of eight feet, padded with button-studded cloth of gold. In recent years Batim has put on some weight and this has blurred the fine profile slightly, but he still remains a remarkably handsome man, his skin colouring southern European, his philosophy somewhat jet set. The drinking started during a year at Oxford and settled into a habit during a very slow world tour from which he returned with considerable reluctance to his native land and a tradition of total abstinence. He got around the tradition by building himself a house well out of the main stream of local life, set back in the foothills of the main range, a mini palace, inspired by Hollywood, not much of it to my taste except perhaps the isolation. To the prince, however, it is as near heaven as he hopes to get, offering now that Islamic promise for the after life of all you want to drink plus girls at the other end of a phone line. He has practically everything including an enormous swimming-pool and a slightly armoured Rolls and no doubt should show signs of the usual discontents of the very rich but doesn't seem to. In so far as I have a function in Batim's patterns it is as a kind of entertainer, someone coming in from the outside world bringing echoes of its bustling which makes an agreeable break in his routine.

I could see plainly enough that tonight he was finding me dull. I talked for half an hour to an almost sullen silence from the bed, and at the end of it he said exactly what I was expecting, which was no, and a bored no at that. He wriggled his toes under the bedcover and added, without looking up :

84

'If you like, Paul, I can give you an introduction to my cousin.'

'Your cousin is of no use to me.'

'Really? Like most politicians he thinks he's of great use to God.'

'I need a Malay in your position who'll come into this as his main thing.'

'My main thing these days is girls. I'm not drinking so much. The family was beginning to make it into a scandal. One of my uncles even suggested packing me off on a pilgrimage to Mecca. A sobering shock, that.'

I looked at the princely opter-out conscious of how much I liked him. There is a segment of my personality which at times positively screams to do exactly what Batim has done so successfully. I said the banal thing.

'You Malays are going to have to wake up.'

'But my dear fellow, we have. Martial law, the army and the police under our hand. We have control.'

'The country's in a state of near panic.'

'Which will pass. With discipline.'

He wriggled his toes again.

'Supposing I let my cousin know what you've told me?' he suggested.

'That would stop a Japanese commercial invasion. I want to make use of it.'

'Is the idea that you play along with these Hawakami people with the object of screwing them in the end?'

'Yes.'

'And why do you want to lose a fat bonus and put yourself to such terrible risk at the same time?'

'If I was trying to jerk a tear I'd say it was for Malaysia. I'm committed to the place.'

'You're more than committed, you've been converted. We Moslems have never gone out to collect converts, they're such a bloody nuisance when you've got them. If I may misquote . . . breathes there a man with soul so dead, who never to himself has said, this is my own, my native Malaysia.'

'That doesn't scan.'

85

'To you it does. Of course, in a way I quite like all this in you. It has a certain beauty. A stand to the death on your adopted heath. In my case if it comes to the death you will find me in St Tropez.'

'Along with all the other refugees from South East Asia?'

'Yes, indeed, but with more money than most of them.'

I didn't think Batim had a vestige of social conscience but a routine check on this was called for.

'All right, you're rich, but what about the ninety-nine and a half per cent of your people who have nothing?'

'To say they have nothing is a misstatement. They had a very good life indeed up until about ten years ago, back in their *kampongs*. They should have stayed in them. It's all this coming to the cities that's caused the trouble.'

'It has happened.'

'Perhaps under our new regime there will be a guided reversal of the process. Back to the simple things.'

'Leaving the Chinese in the towns to grab everything they haven't already got?'

'I refuse to have the Chinese bogey waved at me. We need them up to a point. Under control. We intend to have that control.'

'There is only one kind of control that has any lasting importance these days and that's financial. Governments don't matter a damn.'

'And you saw me as part of this financial power?'

'Why not? You have more brains than anyone else in your pack.'

He smiled.

'How nice of you to say that. It reminds me that some members of what you call the pack were at one time frightened of me. It was why I was sent abroad.'

'Because you had political ambitions?'

He nodded.

'My cousins' side of the family have always been the activists. They didn't fancy competition coming up from our lot, particularly with the brand of doctrine I was offering.'

'What was that?'

'Perhaps you might call it enlightened liberalism. I was

86

very young. However, idealism soon died when I got to the West. Probably from seeing democracy in action. I began to realize that any society which is going to survive requires a disciplined proletariat. Dictatorships really have a lot to be said for them. However, the successful dictator must be at least half-stupid. As you've pointed out, I'm not.'

I stood.

'Mind if I top up my glass?' I asked.

'By all means.'

'You?'

'No, thanks.'

He really did seem to be half on the wagon.

'You haven't finished telling me of your plans, Paul. And I find them most fascinating.'

There was no way of knowing whether he was really interested or simply playing psychiatrist as part of his host duty to a friend. I had nothing to hide from Batim, without him the plan I had fell flat on its face.

'After that play with Min's goons I was at the office until I came here. Setting up a company. Kelantan Developments. I've got two directors, I need two more. You and a Malay stooge, preferably with a title like you.'

He laughed.

'I could pick up a dozen with one phone call. We breed extensively. Let's assume you've got your Malays. What then?'

'You do all the dirty work behind scenes with the people who matter.'

'And just what would that involve?'

'Principally the terms on which the government agrees to let Hawakami, alias Kelantan Developments, have the oil concession.'

'And you have these terms all worked out?'

'More or less. I want them to be a come-on to Hawakami, good enough to start joybells ringing in Tokyo. And as though we had never heard of Pertamina's blackmail. My idea is a five-year contract which ought to give them three years of profit taking if the field turns out all right. The take once the barrels start coming in will be on a fifty-fifty basis, half to the Malay government, half to

Kelantan Developments. I'm pretty certain that Akamoro has been authorized by his home office to go as far as forty-five to them, fifty-five to us. The extra five per cent will bring a happy light into his eyes and it isn't so generous as to make him smell a rat.'

'And this stinking rat?'

'I don't fade when the time comes to make room for those Japanese directors from Tokyo. Nor does Russell. Which leaves Kelantan Developments financed by Japan but with continuing Malay control. Under your Chairmanship.'

'My God! And you?'

There was no doubt now about his interest.

'I'd be a director, voted a salary and fee. I'd lose my second bonus, of course.'

'I should think you'd lose a lot more than that. Hawakami would never forgive you.'

'I know that. But they couldn't force me to commit hara-kiri on a white sheet. And if I left this life under slightly suspicious circumstances you and your board could appoint another Malay to replace me.'

'Listen, Paul, if the Japanese even get a hint of what's in your mind they'll pull out altogether.'

'So what? I'll tell you, the concession goes to someone else, probably a big American company. Hawakami haven't a hope of landing it without me, and they know that. They wouldn't have used me if they could possibly have avoided it. But I don't think there's any danger at all of their finding out what's in my mind because you're the only one in my confidence. Russell Menzies is not and won't be during the preliminary phases. He's an old man now and his nerves aren't as good as they used to be. My idea is to present him with his directorship in Kelantan Developments as a happy birthday present. And I'm not worried about a leak from this room simply because if you play you'll be in the whole thing right up to your neck. If you won't play it was all just a bright idea of mine that got shelved and I'll say so sorry to Mr Akamoro.'

'Your confidence in me is most moving,' Batim said.

'It would be nearer to it to say that I know I couldn't

begin to work this without you close by my side. And all the way. I don't know the first thing about landing a government concession but all you have to do is blackmail the right relation.'

Batim didn't smile.

'What do you do when I say no for the last time?'

'Drive back to Kuala Lumpur and call on Akamoro at his hotel, in spite of the lateness of the hour. And to break his heart. Just when I was beginning to get quite fond of him, too.'

'And then?'

'Hawakami will be out in the cold. And I'll be fighting a diesel engine price war in Manila again.'

'And what about the Chinese company?'

'It would be my hope that you'd speak to your cousin about them and as a result of this that oil in Kelantan would be brought out by an American company. This could be your good deed for the year.'

Suddenly Batim flipped back the cover, swung his legs across the bed, and stood. He was wearing a pale lemon sarong but no shirt and upright a layering of excess flesh, marked while he sprawled against pillows, wasn't so noticeable. He loosened the sarong and then pulled this out tight from his body with both hands, folding it back in again and doing the simple roll over at the top which held it. He walked over to the tray of drinks provided out of courtesy to a guest and poured himself a not too carefully rationed tot which he drank off straight. After that he went back to sit on the edge of the bed and stare at me.

'Tokyo will want to dictate policy to their front company here from round one,' he said.

'What policy? Once we've got that concession we'll be sleeping directors for at least the first year and a half. There won't be a thing for us to do. It'll be over to the technicians and the well sinkers. Oh, we'll have a minimal admin role, but nothing more than that. It's when our role needs to be a lot more than minimal that they'll try to slide their own men on to the board for the takeover. That's when I'm supposed to slide out.'

'So the showdown is then?'

'No. We'll stall them as long as we can. The emotional climate out here isn't yet right for it to be known that finance is all from Japan. Akamoro is nervous about this, very. He won't be difficult to persuade. And don't forget that Hawakami think they found exactly the price for me on one of their computers and paid it. I'm their man. It would never enter their heads that I'd be such a fool as to try to defy them.'

'I can't see this as the road to commercial good health for Harris and Company,' Batim said. 'But of course I know nothing about the competitive life. One thing strikes me, though. Puppet directors refusing to move over to make room for the real owners rather suggests a new variation on the old national expropriation trick.'

'Give me credit for the new variation. And it won't be expropriation, or anything like it.'

'Kinder, you mean?'

'Much kinder.'

Batim shook his head.

'How long do you think you can work this stall of keeping their directors off the board by talk about the weather?'

'With any luck until the concession comes up for renewal in five years. There'll be an earthquake then. But the Japanese are used to these and they're pragmatists. When they see that profits continue to flow to Tokyo on the agreed percentage rate they'll settle down. Also, we'll let them have one director. Perhaps Akamoro.'

Batim sighed.

'The mere idea of presiding over all this disturbs me. Would I be well paid?'

'Very. And outside the country if you want.'

He thought about that. It was perhaps the moment to strike a more idealistic note.

'Batim, you'd be helping to keep a national asset under more or less complete national control. And remember, you'd be chairman. If you felt that this was right policy new concession contracts could favour Malaysia's interests at the expense of Tokyo. Which is the usual thing.'

He smiled.

'I know all about Pertamina, Paul. I do read the papers. And I must say that in many ways what you have outlined is an attractive idea. However, I'm afraid I can't help you at all.'

I emptied my glass.

'You haven't heard my emotional appeal yet,' I said. 'Want it?'

'By all means.'

'I think it's time you did something for your country. You wouldn't have happened to be in K.L. during the rioting?'

'No. But I saw it on television.'

'What you wouldn't see was that they were mostly kids, with no prospects now or in the future. Oil revenues could do a lot for them. And you could see that these were beamed in the right direction.'

'First the man wants me to be chairman of his company, then turn missionary as well. Are you as ambitious as this for all your friends?'

After a moment I said:

'All right, wash out the emotional appeal.'

'I should think so, too. Have you another line of attack?'

'One. You knew I'd try to use you sooner or later?'

He smiled.

'Naturally.'

'I thought you were worth a careful case history.'

'As indeed I am.'

'Amongst other things I found that your grandfather was still exercising his hereditary rights from something like thirty generations back. These included chopping off his subjects' hands for theft and their heads for insubordination.'

'Your researcher slipped up. That was my great-grandfather. And we've moved with the times. I've told you I was practically a liberal for a short time.'

'Batim, your family has a tradition of being highly touchy about any wrong done to it, real or imagined.'

'Granted. But what are you getting at, my dear Paul?'

'In 1943, during the Japanese Occupation, you were

seven. You had a brother of nineteen. He was arrested, first for insulting behaviour towards the conquerors, then charged with sabotage. They didn't know who he was. He didn't tell them. They cut off his head and stuck it on a bamboo pole beside the *padang* in the nearest town. Your family said nothing during or after the war. They went on living in the palace.'

He must have used the carved wooden edge of the bed as a backing for his spring. Before I was out of my chair his hands were at my throat, fingers digging in. He is shorter than I am but his head was back, lips drawn away from his teeth. I looked into the eyes of a Malay *amok*. If he'd come with a knife it would have been between my ribs.

The wrestling went on for seconds, then the clawing at my jugular eased. He broke, turned around, and went back to sit on the edge of the bed, his hands up to his face. His shoulders shook. He was weeping. I knew I had him.

The sound of domestic noise beyond the bedroom woke me. My neck was still sore. There was no morning tea by the bed, which made me look at my watch. It was seven-fifteen. Taro was sitting up on his pad clawing himself with a hind foot. I got up, let the dog out into the garden, then went to the passage. Chong was just coming through the door to Russell's room carrying something in a basin.

'What's happened?'

He took a step or two towards me. His voice was soft.

'Tuan Menzies much sick.'

'I'll phone the doctor.'

'I do. Doctor here.'

'Why didn't you call me?'

'You sleeping . . .'

'Is it Doctor Prentice in there?'

'No. He sick, too. Indian come.'

Prentice's sickness was almost certainly the bottle. The old man should have retired for the specific purpose of drinking himself to death, but he had stubbornly resisted this, claiming that he was one of the few who could stand up to three quarters of whisky on a good day and much more on a bad, though there was increasingly less evidence to support this theory. I kept him because when sober, and even when not, he knew more about tropical medicine than a London based professor of the subject. Prentice leaned heavily on his assistants, so heavily they left him pretty quickly and set up for themselves. The latest assistant was a Tamil, one of the rare pushers amongst his race, for he had somehow got himself to Birmingham and a degree. I had never met the man but he was proving more faithful than the previous European partners in the practice, probably because he had no alternative.

I didn't barge in on a doctor with his patient, but got into a dressing-gown and went out on the main verandah. Chong remembered to bring me a scratch breakfast. I was still at toast and marmalade when a voice said:

'Excuse me. I am Doctor Pargamattam.'

I stood. The man in the white coat with stethoscope around his neck was slight, good looking and very dark. I offered coffee which he accepted and Chong, hovering in the sitting-room, brought a cup and saucer but managed to make it plain that he didn't like a Tamil, even if he was a doctor, using our china.

'How is he?'

Pargamattam shook his head.

'Bad.'

'Heart?'

'Yes.'

'How bad exactly?'

'There is an old-fashioned explanation for the layman.'

'That ought to do me.'

'Fatty degeneration. And the organ is much enlarged.'

'Fifty years of beer intake,' I said.

'Probably. He must be hospitalized. This morning. I wish to make the arrangements. I'm wondering if Mr Menzies is on some nursing scheme?'

'No. He didn't apply until he was already breaking up. They wouldn't have him.'

'I see. Then what about a private room?'

'Everything. Private nurses. He can afford it.'

'I'll phone the hospital.'

'Is he going to live?'

'Who can say? In these cases you never know. But if he gets over this he may go on for years. Needing care always, I'd say.'

I considered my house with Russell back in it needing care all the time, deciding that a cute Chinese nurse wouldn't upset things too much, though it looked as though this might be the end of our social life. That didn't sadden me as a prospect.

It was twenty minutes before the doctor reappeared.

'The ambulance is coming. I have a room at the hospital. He wishes to see you, Mr Harris.'

'Ought I to?'

'For a few minutes.'

Even very fat men seem to shrink quickly in acute illness. Russell's colour had never been good, pasty until the artificial beer flush arrived, and though there was still a sizable mound under the cover his shrivelled face said that during the night he had been very near death and hadn't yet moved far back from it. It may have been partly the way he was lying, propped up with pillows, his head sunk into them, nested in foam padding, but he was already almost unrecognizable and I couldn't give much for his chances. His eyes were open but the lids crumpled down as though the balls had contracted and were now too small for their sockets.

'I'm sorry about this, Russell.'

It wasn't much to say. I couldn't think of anything else. What I really wanted then was him out of the house, catered for in a place geared to deal with the wrecks we all become. I'm not a natural nurse. Wounds don't worry me, I can cope with them all right, but I'm inclined to turn from debility of Russell's kind, to leave it to people who are qualified for the job. Whenever I've been in a bad way myself all I wanted was to be left alone with professionals, not burdened by a need to make an effort towards those who had brought to my bedside nothing more than a troubled helplessness. We tend to forget this about

94

the gravely ill, that they have moved on to a different plane of experience, often away on journeys in the mind which they don't really want to have interrupted.

But Russell didn't seem to be travelling, his stare was intent enough. His lips moved. I went closer to the bed. He moved a hand on top of the cover, but only a flutter. He hadn't the strength to raise it.

'Wanted . . . son. But . . . not . . . marriage . . .'

The corners of his lips lifted, his mouth opened and stayed that way for seconds. It was a completely soundless laugh.

'If you're saying you adopted me, Russell, I don't believe it.'

'True. All . . . I've . . . got . . .'

Maybe I should have bent down and kissed him, but I didn't. The ambulance arrived and men with a stretcher took over while I waited in the sitting-room and then, somehow not wanting to see Russell carried through the place he had made his own, I went out across the porch and down on to the lawn.

The usual services were apparently getting back to norm in Kuala Lumpur. The Malay driver leaned against his vehicle, not acknowledging me, just gazing down at gravel. He spat, then ground this waste through stones towards the clay soil under them. The doors of the ambulance were swung back and the spacious, steely emptiness inside suggested a car ferry stern in to a dock waiting its load. I could smell hospital.

Russell was brought down steps strapped on a stretcher with a blanket up to his nose. His eyes were shut. The ambulance men were feeling his weight a bit and shouted for the driver to come and give them a hand. I went forward but before I could help the load was stowed.

Pargamattam came up behind me on the way to his car.

'Perhaps he will live,' the doctor said.

CHAPTER VI

A BLACK-BEARDED white-turbaned Sikh six feet tall is a conspicuous figure any place and mightn't seem the best type to employ for a bit of quiet snooping but actually Bahadur made quite effective use of what can only be called race cover in jobs of this kind. Certainly he was always spotted, but after an incident all that witnesses could say was that a Sikh had been on the scene, totally unable to offer police or others interested a more detailed identification. From a distance, and even fairly close up, Sikhs look remarkably alike. Old ones dye their beards which makes an age assessment difficult, too. Nor can these people really be fitted into any social niche in the societies they inhabit, some Sikhs in Malaysia are itinerant pedlars riding around on bikes with two-wheeled trailers behind selling junk in the *kampongs*, others are highly successful department-store owners to be seen climbing in and out of their chauffeur-driven Jaguars. In between are an assortment of lawyers, doctors, traffic cops, and eating-stall proprietors.

I knew that Bahadur would have turned up at the Grand Hotel for his assignment of keeping an eye on Akamoro looking like the better class of commercial traveller from Singapore on a selling mission. The booking clerk would see another Sikh who could only be classified by his suiting which would be a nicely pressed two-piece finished off with hand-made shoes. Nor would the fact that while in the hotel my assistant kept very much to himself cause any interest. Sikhs tend to do this. Their religion keeps them out of cocktail bars and a natural reserve in public is an almost unbroken rule, they talk to their own kind, or when selling, but otherwise isolate themselves in a positive cocoon of withdrawal from the adjacent ungodly.

The man earns what I pay him and is simply biding his time until his involvement in my affairs has become so deep I more or less have to offer him that directorship, changing our name to Harris, Bahadur and Company. At this point he'll marry to make sure there is an heir to the business.

He rang me at exactly half-past nine and his reaction to the news that Russell had been taken to hospital was completely non-emotional. The two hadn't met often and Russell had been disapproving of his appointment, saying that he had made it a lifetime principle never to use Sikhs for anything.

'Has anything happened with you?' I asked.

'Nothing too much.'

'What does that mean?'

'Well, last night a British woman came to the hotel. I was quite near the desk when she signed in. I heard her tell the clerk that she couldn't spend another night alone in her house. The rioting had frightened her. She was carrying a dressing-case and a portable radio.'

'What time was this?'

'After ten. She went straight to her room. Later I was able to see the register. The name was Mrs Thomas Johnson.'

'What did she look like?'

'Blonde. Straight hair. Too thin. Her eyes were a very deep blue.'

This was not good news.

'Have you seen her since?'

'Yes. Ten minutes ago she came downstairs with her radio and went out to sit by the pool.'

'So?'

'The pool is where Mr Akamoro does his morning Judo exercises. He eats only a light breakfast before them. He is wearing swimming shorts so I expect he will use the pool afterwards. In spite of his exercises he has too fat a stomach.'

'Is there anyone else out there?'

'Not when I came away to phone.'

'Is the girl near Akamoro?'

'No. She was in a cabana chair half-way along, he was at the top of the pool lying on his belly and pulling his legs backwards. She has the radio on very loud. I think perhaps this disturbs the Japanese.'

'Keep an eye on them but don't be seen doing it. I'm coming down. Fast. Am I right, isn't there a lane beside the hotel that runs up past the pool and ends in a blind?'

'Yes. The pool's screened from it by a hibiscus hedge.'

'I'll come up the lane. If you see any kind of action, join me.'

'Yes, Mr Harris.'

I got into clothes and ran for the Mini. A man is vulnerable in swimming trunks, even if he has been practising his Judo. From what I'd seen of Akamoro's physical condition exercise of any kind would be more likely to wind him than set him up for unarmed combat. The little car was hard to start, as though yesterday's strain on it had oiled up a plug. She was still sparking badly as I got her down the drive and there was more exhaust than there should have been. I've always been careful about servicing the Mercedes but this box tends to be forgotten.

On the flat the car protested seriously, acceleration nothing like what it should have been. I was held up by two traffic lights and a policeman back on point work after riot duty, surly from this. An imperious white-gloved hand held me up for a long time. Then I got behind a builder's lorry on a narrow street with a lot of traffic coming at us. It took me fifteen minutes to reach the Grand Hotel.

I wasn't totally surprised to see a Citroen Safari parked empty well up the lane, and past the service entrance. It had backed in and was facing down towards me. I drove the Mini up, yanked on the handbrake and jumped out. The Citroen's escape route was blocked.

The morning was being blasted by Chinese hot jazz from a Singapore station. There was no actual entrance to the pool from that lane and I ran along a hedge in bright flower to a point where it had been penetrated, and with no respect for preserving amenity. I went through where other men had recently gone through before me and saw them at once.

The attack had just started. Three characters in golfing

98

caps were towing Akamoro along tiling. I saw trousered legs sticking out from a cabana chair but the girl in there wasn't disturbed at all. There was no sign of Bahadur.

Akamoro was certainly doing a valiant best, but it was a long time since he had earned his black belt, and his current best wasn't all that good. Two of his assailants had a leg each for towing and a third was reducing the effectiveness of the Japanese's arm action by putting in well-placed kicks. I couldn't hear any yowling above the noise from the radio. Under those caps the three thugs were dressed for action in what looked like cotton track suits, Chinese with eccentric gymnast training.

One of them saw me and dropped a leg. Bahadur came at the run up the side of the pool. Something told me he wasn't going to get past that cabana chair and he didn't. There was a splash just audible above the jazz.

Two of the thugs jumped me. It was a fine piece of teamwork from long practice, synchronized arm and leg action. I stayed on my feet for a commendable number of seconds, then joined Akamoro on tiling. On the way down I saw that Bahadur had made the mistake of trying to get out of the pool near the action site and was pushing his body up from hands flat out on a concrete edging. Akamoro's thug moved over to step on them. From flat on my stomach I saw the Sikh go back into the water. He had lost his turban and long black hair mixed with his beard. I got a kick in the ribs and then a second, which ruled me out for a moment as an observer though I did have an impression of Akamoro starting to crawl towards the water. I think a foot on his neck stopped that.

The three gymnasts gave me their total attention. I writhed in the lift, but it still went on, like college rough play without the laughter. They swung me back twice, achieving a nice rhythmic balance, then spun me from their hands. I went over water like a circus stunt man shot from a cannon, or that's the way it felt. I had time en route to see a blonde's trousered legs up to the thigh. They were crossed.

When I surfaced Akamoro was engaged in a surprising rally. He had run for it while his attackers dealt with me,

99

not back towards the hotel via that argument against the emancipation of women, but up to the top of the pool and had now turned to face his pursuers, a little man well established in middle life with a pot, but still endowed with a national spirit that has made his people ready to defy apparently hopeless odds. He was using his arms like a competitor in a rice-husking championship, and if they had made contact with anything there might have been a real shift in the balance of power, but they were only hitting air. I realized why. He had lost his glasses and without them was three parts blind. Those bastards knew it, too, and were simply waiting for the man to tire himself.

Bahadur was swimming for the top of the pool, black locks streaming behind him. I made for the lady, I could see her now, and there was no question of mistaken identity. She reached down and without rising took off a sandal, holding this in her hand with the wooden wedge thrust forward for use as a weapon. I'd hate to be a burglar in her house.

When Jean Hyde stood I thought it was to receive me, but it wasn't, she had noticed a development the rest of us were missing. Someone must have looked out of a hotel bedroom and raised the alarm for down at the lower end of the pool were three waiters and what could be the manager, or his assistant, armed with a shotgun. He didn't hesitate to use it, either, almost as though he had been waiting for the right moment all through the riots. There was a bang and then another, and the gun seemed aimed roughly in the direction of three athletes and a half-naked Japanese whom they were now in the act of prising through a hedge. The thugs reaction to bullets was immediate, they left their victim and went through the flowering shrubs without him.

I tried to bellow a message to our relief forces but this didn't get through the sound of jazz from the portable Jean was now carrying as she ran. She was also making a noise, the wailing of a girl who has just been through a traumatic experience that is going to haunt her for years.

Bahadur and I got out of the pool at different spots almost at the same time. We both ran towards that hole in the hibiscus hedge. Akamoro was sitting on his bottom this side of it looking like a plump infant who has fallen out of its pram and is still too stunned to howl.

From the lane came the sound of a car pile up. It was my car and the Citroen. Both were in motion, the snout of the French job pushing my box down the lane, simply bulldozing an obstacle ahead of it, and with a wild engine revving, the Mini being scraped along on locked wheels. The Citroen's exhaust cloud looked like a jet's in the first steep climb.

The driver of the Citroen saw us coming. He took the offensive at once, slamming into reverse, breaking contact with the Mini and coming back up the lane fast in a zigzag designed to send us back through the hibiscus hedge again. Bahadur and I didn't go right through it, we struck a thick patch, but amongst all that foliage lost vision. What I heard was another gear change, a whine of acceleration, then seconds later a very loud crash. We clawed our way out of cover.

My Mini had been pushed up a couple of steps and practically into the service entrance and two now stationary cars seemed hopelessly locked together. Then there was the noise of sheet metal giving way to intense pressure, followed by a blue exhaust screen through which I saw a chrome bumper that belonged to me rise in the air. A small bonnet lid bounced up on its hinges followed by a loud crunching. The Citroen broke through dragging pieces of clanking metal, some of which was theirs, some mine. I was left with the second write-off of the week.

The escaping car went into a noisy left turn around the bulk of the hotel and disappeared. The service entrance was blocked. We both turned and ran back up beside the hedge, reaching the major hole through it just as the hotel executive came bouncing out into the lane, with shotgun at the ready. I didn't stay to talk to him, practically jumping over Akamoro who was still on tiling, then running along the edge of the pool towards the hotel. For a moment it looked as though one of the waiters was going to tackle me but he thought better of it.

The reception clerk had remained at his post. He didn't like a dripping man collapsing over his clean blotter.

'That girl . . .? Mrs Johnson . . .?'

He kept dignity.

'The lady has left the hotel. By taxi.'

I didn't bother looking for the taxi. I should have given the clerk the Citroen's number for a phone in to the police, but I didn't bother with that either. These were troubled days and a slight fracas at an hotel, even involving attempted kidnapping, wasn't going to excite the area superintendent much.

When I got back to the pool Akamoro was being inspected for damage, something that seemed to interest him too. Before I reached the cabana chair he was installed in it, surrounded by an interested crowd. The hotel executive had put down his shotgun and was in charge, a man meeting crisis with resolution and firmness. It was more than I could claim for myself.

Bahadur was standing a little apart, a wet Sikh. Black hair plastered against his skull and pasted down on his chest somehow stripped him of his usual defences against the world and he looked both very young and rather lost.

'We neither of us deserve the Malaysia Star for this action,' I said.

Suddenly the boy grinned. This happens rarely but whenever it does I get the feeling that we may evolve a human relation yet, given plenty of time, perhaps even coming to that partnership so long as he is kept very junior during my active span.

His turban was floating on the pool, about five yards of the kind of fine cambric you can draw through a wedding ring. We both looked at it.

'I'm getting out of here,' I said, keeping my voice lower than was necessary. 'I want you to have Akamoro at Yung Ching Wa's at half-past seven tonight, with his suitcases. I don't care how you do it but you're both arriving without a tail. That's important.'

Bahadur nodded. The hotel executive turned to me.

'Your name, please?'

'Paul Harris. And if I'm wanted for questioning later the police know where I live. At the moment I have an appointment.'

'You must come to the office to wait for investigation!'

'To hell with that,' I said, and made for the hedge.

At the gap I looked back, but he hadn't picked up the shotgun.

The taxi hit heavy midtown traffic and took a long time to get me home. I sat in clothes that seemed to be drying stiff, possibly from the chlorine in the pool.

Min Kow Lin were certainly showing a flexibility in opposition which one doesn't really expect from a large corporation with a glass skyscraper head office. It was obvious that they were totally contemporary in outlook, right in there with the new thing. Kidnapping as an instrument in commercial warfare is probably a perfectly logical development from the games a number of us have been playing in recent years, and particularly out in these parts, but the first time you hit its applied use personally there is a certain shock factor, even a sense of outrage.

It was perfectly easy to see what they were up to. Either Akamoro or me, preferably both, set gently to one side just at this time, would be advantage to Min in a very big way. We could be quietly detained at a remote rubber estate or vegetable farm in the Cameron Highlands for as long as it took Min to negotiate for and finally secure a government mineral exploitation concession over a considerable area of southern Kelantan. I was pretty certain they did not know I was in contact with Batim Salong in this matter for I'd been careful to take evasive action in that night drive to the Tunku's rural hideout. As Min saw things the solution to their problem was a couple of snatches. In my case they knew that a disappearance wasn't going to cause much excitement because I've rather made a habit of dropping out of the local picture from time to time without leaving a forwarding address. Tokyo would be very unhappy about a missing executive but Min were probably counting on Hawakami not wanting publicity since this would involve a beam focused on them that could be embarrassing in the extreme. There was also the fact that people do vanish rather too frequently in Malaysia, public opinion geared to accept this.

I didn't think I'd have been killed or mistreated, just held as a prisoner of commercial war, finally released as the result of a belated ransom demand that I hoped my accountant would have decided to pay, with nothing in all this to point a finger at Min. And if I tried to do some finger pointing when I got free the result would be a million dollar slander suit.

The fact that two kidnap attempts had been muffed didn't rule out further attempts. Akamoro simply could not be left lying around loose in Kuala Lumpur while I was up north. I needed Bahadur with me which meant that he wouldn't be available as a bodyguard of the second class. The only safe place for my Japanese colleague was with Batim Salong.

While I had a shower and changed I thought about the Tunku's probable reaction to my suggestion. It was unlikely to be warm. It was so cold that I thought for minutes that we were going to lose our new Chairman. It took a long time, hampered by the caution needed over a wire, to do the persuading, and I think he only capitulated because he had suddenly become really interested in the oil project. Maybe all these years Batim had only been waiting for the chance to get into something big right at the top. There were clear signs now that he had no intention of just being a figurehead and that was all right by me.

After Batim I rang the hospital. Russell had undergone an emergency operation for an embolism an hour before and was still in the recovery-room. The official handout was that everything had gone fine though, of course, at his age there was a certain unpredictable shock factor. I read that as preparing me for the news in the next hour or so that the old man was dead, and suddenly I felt low.

Out in the sitting-room with a can of beer in my hand I felt worse. The house seemed enormous and empty. The servants were in a withdrawal phase, shut away in the retreat of the kitchen. There were no sounds and dust on flat surfaces said the morning had gone by without cleaning. I thought of Russell's files in a locked bookcase I could open easily enough and knew that it would be a long time before I went into that room to consult them. Taro sat by my chair trying to blackmail me with sighs into taking him for a walk, but without much hope.

He barked before I heard the crunch of tyres on the drive. When the bell rang he barked again and I told him to shut up. I could have gone to the door myself but waited to see if we still had service. Chong's ballet feet came hissing down the corridor.

'Is Mr Harris at home?'

I didn't at once recognize the voice, it was low.

'Yes, Mem.'

'I'd like to see him.'

I went out into the hall. Ruth Potter was still on the verandah as though, in spite of having asked for me, she wasn't sure about coming in.

'You're just in time for a drink.'

I told her what had happened to Russell. She made noises, but was abstracted, as though the removal of someone else's embolism just couldn't reach her in imagination at all. She was pale and hadn't been careful about her make-up. I gave her a gin.

'I shouldn't have come here, I know.'

'Why not?'

'Well, it's not your business at all. It's just that . . .'

'Just what, Ruth?'

'I wanted to know . . . how a man would react. And you were the nearest. That's about it.'

A cigarette trembled in her fingers as I lit it. She looked up at me.

'Am I being talked about?'

'What?'

'Oh, you know, in places like men's room, bars . . .'

'I'm just not with you?'

'Paul, do you really mean that? You don't know? You hadn't heard?'

'About what?'

'Archie.'

I thought of what I had heard about Archie recently. It didn't tot up to much.

'He has a mistress. A Chinese. He's set her up. Right here in this town. In a flat.'

'Ruth, are you quite sure this isn't just talk?'

'It's talk all right, but not just. I could give you the address. It was given to me.'

'You haven't done anything about that?'

'No.'

What to say to her? That after seventeen years of marriage these things happen? A lot of good that would do. I felt sorry for her, and not in the way that a lot of her friends would be feeling sorry for her. There was a certain gallantry in sticking to a marriage with someone like Archie. I liked her much better than I did him. She was considerably more intelligent for one thing, for another she had a kind of persistent gaiety which isn't a bad way to face the contemporary world, even if it's an act. At the same time I could see that she wouldn't make things easy for Archie in their private patterns largely because it was improbable that she had a remnant of respect for him left. A Chinese girl, if she was stupid enough, would be ego building and the fool probably fancied himself as a sexual athlete inhibited by the wrong woman at home.

Ruth was staring at me.

'I'm broad-minded,' she said. 'I mean, I really am! There are things I wouldn't mind, that I knew happened. Like when he was in Penang or somewhere. A call girl. All men do it.'

I wasn't quite sure whether or not I was expected to confirm this statement.

'Oh, Paul, it's in this town, and everyone knowing. I mean we're all in each other's pockets. Some of them have even seen the girl. I know what she looks like. One of the really pretty Chinese. I wonder what she sees in him?'

'Money.'

After a moment Ruth said:

'Thank you for that.'

'I meant it. You haven't said anything to Archie?'

'No.'

'How long have you known?'

'Three days. Paul I . . . I seemed to have come to an arrangement with my life. You know what I mean?'

'Yes.'

'Archie's Archie and always will be. I knew that. But . . . well, I had a good deal. I mean in the old-fashioned sense. Count your blessings and all that. And I liked the life out here. It's much more interesting than anything we'd have had in England. In fact I just don't like to think about going back there. Now I have to. I probably ought to take the children and just go.'

'Don't do anything dramatic.'

'Paul, don't you see? I've said I don't mind his casual girls. That didn't really hit at me at all. It's his planning *this*, arranging it, a kind of permanent alternative.'

'I wouldn't call it permanent.'

'That's the way he sees it. And he must have known that people would find out sooner or later, in this town sooner. The talk was bound to get back to me.'

'It's possible Archie didn't think that, imagined he could be smart.'

'If that's consolation I don't like its taste. And anyway we're going to blow up over this when it comes out between us. I'm not taking it and I'm going to tell him so. I know how Archie reacts when he's cornered, he goes into a really filthy rage in which he'll say anything. This time he'll say the final thing.'

'Not if you handle him right.'

'Oh, God, no! This isn't something I can handle. I'm not going to be reasonable. I can't. I feel as if I'd been walked on somehow. I know I'm not being contemporary about this. I should take a lover myself. Renew my own damn youth. Well, I don't want to. And it's not that I expected an awful lot, either, I just thought that we'd made something in a kind of way. Small, maybe, but something that wouldn't be damaged. I suppose it was based on the feeling he needed me. Now I know he doesn't.'

'You don't know anything of the sort.'

'A man who needs a woman considers her enough to save her face. I've been in the East long enough to believe in face saving. I think it's part of living. It's something you've got to serve other people, if they're close to you in any way. Archie hasn't served me that. He's made me a joke in this town.'

'I still haven't heard that joke in a men's room.'

'You will. You're away a lot.'

'Ruth, if your mind is made up why come to see me?'

'I didn't want to see another woman.'

She tried a laugh.

'Look, I can't give you advice, I've no qualifications to do that. About all I can manage is to raise one or two points if you want to hear them?'

'Yes, I do.'

'Had you thought about telling Archie what you've just told me . . . call girls tolerable, a second establishment not.'

She stared.

'What? Tell Archie *that*?'

'All I'm saying is that it's a possible approach to the situation. Whether it would work is another matter. You'd have to think about that.'

'What approach?'

'Keeping it hard and light and no tears.'

'Why, you . . .' She stopped.

'If you were going to say I'm on Archie's side I'm glad you didn't. I don't mind having a drink with him sometimes but I can't stand his jokes.'

'God, neither can I!'

I took her glass and went over to fill it again. She needed the gin even if she was driving. While I was still at the side table she called out:

'Paul, what are you really trying to tell me?'

'Just that it might be an angle to raise the practical aspects of this thing. The future for both of you. Archie's in employment that only brings a modest pension. I've never heard that either of you have much money of your own, which means it's about time you both started to consider what is going to happen when you get older. Running two establishments is no way to save.'

'You think I could be so splendidly cold-blooded?'

'I don't know. And I'm not suggesting that you try. It only seemed to me something that just might work with Archie.'

I brought her glass back. She took it and had more than a sip.

'Your idea is that I deliver an ultimatum laughing?'

'I wouldn't make it more than a smile.'

Ruth didn't stay very long after that. While she was still with me I had the feeling I'd lost any credits I'd built up with her, and when the front door shut and a car crunched away I sat down thinking that I'd been an utter fool to trot out those glib suggestions. She'd been in desperate need of some kind of positive and I'd produced one, but I couldn't begin to think it was a useful positive.

Who the hell would volunteer to be a marriage counsellor? They must be half-crazed with self-importance.

CHAPTER VII

I spent the afternoon waiting for a call from the hospital. It didn't come. At four I rang them. Russell was back in his private room, under heavy sedation. His progress was satisfactory, but it was improbable that he would be able to have visitors for at least the next day or two, and it might be a week before he was noticing the world around him again. In view of this it didn't seem too heartless to leave town. I would order a florist to send flowers. Russell never noticed flowers, but I couldn't send him beer.

Chong appeared to ask if I would be home for dinner. I said no but made no mention of impending travels. The man looked thinner than ever, his face drawn. I wondered if he felt anything like real affection for Russell. There was no way of knowing.

I was in my bedroom packing what I would need into a rucksack when the phone rang and my heart jumped.

'Dale Mostin here. Is that you, Paul?'

'Yes.'

'I just got back from Ipoh after lunch. We had our

showroom windows broken up there. Nothing much but I had to see to it. That's why I've been so long in ringing you.'

'About what?'

'I wouldn't have thought the owner of a burned up Mercedes would wonder why a car dealer was contacting him.'

'You know about that?'

'I not only know about it, yesterday morning I identified a lump of metal at the city dump for the police.'

'Why did they need you?'

'Because the back licence plate had melted and the front one seemed to have been wrenched off as a souvenir.'

'You identified my car by its engine number?'

'That's right.'

'When you sold me insurance on that Mercedes, Dale, I don't remember your saying anything about riot cover?'

It was a moment before he spoke.

'Look, I feel sick about this. The fact is I haven't been recommending riot cover. It puts so much on the premium that with things as quiet as they have been it seemed to make sense to skip it.'

'I'd be interested to know if your plate glass in Ipoh was covered?'

'That's a building, it's different. Paul, I know you could kill me. I want to do what I can. I'll cut my dealer's profit right out on anything new you buy.'

'You think I can afford to buy new?'

'Go on, grind my face in the dirt.'

'What I had in mind was a personally recommended used job. Got anything interesting?'

He thought for a moment.

'How would a two months old Ford Zodiac do? About seven-fifty on the clock. It belonged to a man who's been posted to Zambia and he left it with me to sell. Like new, I promise. I'll cut my commission and let you have seven-fifty dollars off the new list price. A real bargain.'

'A Zodiac is much bigger than I had in mind.'

'But you've got your Mini?'

'Not any more. I should think it's at the city dump,

too. Towed away from beside the Grand Hotel. Not exactly a riot casualty, but it'll pass for that in these days.'

'You mean it's a total write-off, too?'

'It looked very much that way to me.'

'My God, when was this?'

'Today.'

'What have you been getting up to?'

'I never get up to anything. Things just happen to me.'

'So you've no transport?'

'Well, a bicycle. But my cook needs that. How about a smaller Ford, something like a Cortina? I'm considering packing in prestige cars, they're too conspicuous for our time.'

'I haven't such a thing in the place. Look, I'm sure you're going to like this Zodiac. Run it around for a week. Be my guest.'

'Make that two weeks and including a personal delivery by you to the lane behind Yung Ching Wa's by nine o'clock this evening. With a full tank and the ignition key in an envelope which you will give to the restaurant doorman. You will then go home as unobtrusively as you got the car out of your showrooms and drove it downtown.'

'What is all this, Paul?'

'A customer's whim. Pander to it and you may find me smiling the next time we meet at the Golf Club. Which will mean that I'm still using the same car dealer.'

'Will do,' Dale said.

He was keen. You have to be if you want to keep the Ford franchise and sell Mercedes as well.

Taro had seen me packing the haversack and was now looking as a dog does on these occasions. He came along to the sitting-room, but without real hope of a quiet evening watching television and almost as soon as it was dark I left the lights burning, going back to the bedroom which stayed unlit while I gathered up what was needed. Taro went to his pad. I didn't try to console him with promises, he doesn't believe in them any more.

The moon hadn't come up and there was plenty of black shadow outside. I skirted the lawn and then where this ended and woods began, paused to listen, hearing nothing but traffic noises from below the hill. I didn't really think that Min would have watchers on my house, for one thing they would have found out about the dog, for another after two snatch bids that hadn't come off it seemed likely they would be pausing for a re-think. But I still didn't take any chances and went nowhere near the drive, moving slowly down through my hardwoods to the perimeter fence which had once been electrified. That idea had been to protect my privacy but it hadn't worked and I'd scrapped the thing. Mosquito oilers had since made several convenient holes in it and I used one of these, reaching town level in about twenty minutes, taking another fifteen to get to a street in which there were taxis roving again as a kind of proclamation that our troubles were behind us.

Yung Ching Wa's always give me the same room. It is on the third floor, reached by a wobbly lift, and is more than vaguely reminiscent of a suburban police cell mainly used for sobering up drunks. The way the proprietor feels about this is that if you don't like his cement and plaster decor you can eat somewhere else and be damned to you for a fool.

I sat down on a bench that was as uncompromising as purgatory, smoking a cigar while I waited. Unfolding Lotus brought my whisky, a giggly, plump girl, whose big line, which she had worked out all by herself, was patting customers with her fat little hands when there was any reasonable excuse to do this and quite often when there wasn't. Tonight her hands were smelling slightly of onions from some auxiliary work in the kitchens. An American had taught her to call all men 'Lover' and she had taken to that with great zest. It sometimes startled new patrons.

My guests were twenty minutes late and when they showed up Akamoro was looking as though he now wished his countrymen had never gone snooping for oil in Kelantan. The areas of facial skin which Bahadur exposed were flushed, but this could have been from carrying two outsize suitcases. Whisky did Akamoro some good, though I felt sorry for the Sikh with his orange squash. He didn't respond too well to being patted, either.

I refused to talk until we had eaten and by the time

our slab table was loaded Akamoro's interest in living had returned. He stripped chopsticks from their paper with the expression of a man on the verge of religious ceremonial and ten minutes later was using those bits of wood to test sauces, dabbing pieces of duck in side dishes and then flipping these dripping to his mouth. For some time Bahadur just sat there as though certain that none of this was Sikh kosher, but after the first tentative experiments he stopped worrying about getting gravy on his beard. We were all Orientals, with manners to match, and it wasn't long before I began to get wonderful guest tribute noises directed towards a host, suckings, hisses and finally the awaited, reverberating belches of pure joy. After thirty minutes or so Akamoro said with convincing simplicity:

'Oh! Most good!'

'You have to pay for it, just in case you thought I was trying to entertain you on the cheap.'

'This meal worthy of kings.'

We had been drinking whisky straight through. Whatever the Chinese may say they don't have a drinkable wine and European ones all find themselves in conflict with the contrast sauces. You can have beer with Chinese food if you must, and lager if you've never had much of a palate anyway, but for the purist only the Scotch produce is really possible, with water, not too much, and certainly no ice. Whisky seems to do for rice-based food just exactly what it does for its own native haggis, providing a gastronomic accompaniment that is firm and positive but never intrusive.

By the time we had reached the green tea stage Akamoro's eyes were shining and there were pink areas in his cheeks. If I weren't a realist I could almost have believed he loved me. Unfolding Lotus came in to clear away the debris and when she finally left there remained on the table a tea pot, three hideous porcelain cups, two glasses and a half-empty bottle of the blend I tend to ask for when I don't want a malt. We were now ready for our planning conference. I spread out the ordnance map with Akamoro's circle on it.

'Kelantan Developments should be a registered limited

liability company within a week,' I said. 'His Excellency the Tunku is already at work in his own way on the concession project. I can't say when he'll get this through, it's the sort of thing that takes time, but we needn't worry about that because with Batim Salong on the job up where it matters we have Min stalled dead. Batim's first task is to find out whether Min has already applied for the concession, though I think it is very unlikely that they have done this yet.'

Akamoro lit a cigarette. After the meal he'd just had and in view of steady progress towards mutual understanding I thought we might have reached the Paul and Ken stage, but the Japanese wasn't rushing anything.

'Mr Harris, Min Kow Lin intelligence service most good. You think it possible to conceal for much longer that His Excellency the Prince assists us?'

'No, I don't.'

'They find out, what then?'

'It would be nice to think they'd chuck the whole business and leave the field to us. But I don't believe they will. They'd still be second in the running. And if anything should happen to you and me Batim isn't in this far enough yet to carry on by himself. They'll see that. And they might try a deal of some kind, stepping forward with an organization already geared for oil exploitation. In any other country but this one Min would have had a highly paid government lobby all dug in which we couldn't have begun to fight. We're lucky there. The troubles happen to be working for us, against them.'

Akamoro smiled.

'You and I must take great care of our health in immediate future.'

'That's why I'm not going to Kelantan by road or public transport. My boat's at Kuantan and I'm using it. You've guessed you're going to stay with the Tunku?'

He nodded.

'Experience should be most useful for me.'

For them both.

'I've told Batim Salong we want him as chairman of the new company.'

Akamoro sat up straight.

'I do not understand? Surely you are right man?'

'No. We want an impressive figurehead. I don't think I am.'

'This man impresses so much?'

'I think he'll learn to. Quickly.'

'Tokyo will not approve!'

'Akamoro, you're the man on the spot. You're telling Hawakami in this matter, and you know it. And if I'm to fade on schedule to make room for new blood it's better that I'm not sitting at the head of the table when the time comes to do that. You'll have a Malay prince in the chair and who can say then that the country's best interests aren't being served?'

Akamoro thought about this. I couldn't guess what Bahadur was thinking about. The Sikh was leaning back on the bench seat apparently digesting his meal as he gazed at a wall. I hoped he appreciated being included in on this discussion. I was taking a calculated risk sooner than I had intended with the man, one that would leave me very exposed indeed if he suddenly decided that the moment had arrived for him to branch out on his own. His check up on Min in Kuala Lumpur had produced nothing at all, not even a hint that the Chinese corporation had organized a Land-Rover safari to accompany John Hyde north. In the past he had proved a pretty good snooper, though this morning I'd had the feeling that he had come very near to achieving neutrality. I knew that Min would pay very good money for a spy in my camp.

'Bahadur, I want you to go up to Kelantan via the Trengganu coast road. I suggest your motor bike. You can play it any way you like. Your job is to find out exactly where Hyde is, what he is doing, then report to me on my boat. We'll be tied up north of Kota Bharu in the Kelantan River. At *Kampong* Sintang. You'll find it easily enough.'

'All right,' he said.

Akamoro looked at Bahadur then, as though until this moment he had been taking the Sikh on trust as part of my organization and was now wondering whether he should have done. These twitches of suspicion are a regular part of the patterns at executive level and when they stop happening it means you're just about due for that note in the annual prospectus which says how much the company is going to miss your wise guidance in the years that lie ahead.

I decided to postpone discussing my first task in Kelantan until Akamoro and I were alone in the Zodiac. Dale Mostin had done his job all right and we got the car key from the doorman to find a large grey model parked in the lane. Bahadur, acting as porter, packed the bags in the boot, then took an unemotional farewell of us both. I drove around downtown streets for a time, and after that some suburban ones, doing routine checks for a tail but picking up nothing suspicious in the mirror. I wished, though, that the Ford's rear lighting arrangements hadn't been quite so distinctive, uneasily conscious of our backside as brightly illumined as a bar entrance. However, when we got on the Seremban road the night traffic was thin and at ninety-seven on a long straight I shook off all following headlights.

I was beginning to think that Dale was right and I would like the Zodiac. If I kept it the springing would need to be tightened for my kind of cornering, a fractional surrender of comfort for performance, but at speed the car kept me happy enough, beginning to seem value for money.

'You leave for Kelantan immediately, Mr Harris?'

'As soon as I've handed you over to Batim.'

'To travel by your ship takes some time?'

'Not really. She's fast. Also, she provides me with a comfortable base from which to operate. Like our generals.'

'Excuse please?'

'Probably your Japanese generals didn't use them, but ours tended to go in for their own fitted caravans. The planners need their little comforts.'

'What is your plan?'

'To buy that Klampa estate at once. And at almost any price. Do you think Tokyo will agree?'

'Yes.'

He sounded just slightly surly.

116

'I hope you're right and Min haven't got hold of it already.'

'Most unlikely.'

'Could we still work that oil field if Min owned the rubber?'

'Oil reservoir some distance from estate.'

'But supposing there is just one little bay of that slime lake running back under Klampa estate rubber? What would stop Min from racing us to get a derrick up and start pumping before we could? Believe me, if they've bought the estate they'll have the minerals rights under it.'

'I think you worry without need.'

'I hope so.'

'Mr Harris, there is careful investigation by us of present owner. He is simple man who wishes family property and quiet living.'

The poor devil was going to have that dream exploded if it hadn't been already.

'This was some time ago,' I said. 'And we're in the oil business now. You just stop short of murder, and sometimes not even that.'

'You are alarmist.'

'That's not my word for it. Mr Akamoro, please stay tucked away where I'm taking you.'

'I will,' he said. 'Communication between us now impossible for some time?'

'Not at all. My boat is fitted with radio telephone. And His Excellency has an unlisted Seremban number. We can chat any time we like.'

My boat had been built more or less to my own designs by a Scottish yard and I had justified her appalling cost on the grounds that I needed a fast little job which could take me out on quick visits to my junk fleets. But I had only used her once for this purpose and as executive transport the *Tanjong Pudu* wasn't bringing in much return for capital investment. The things you love never do.

A special relation between me and my boat had sprung to life the first time I stepped on her deck planking when she was moored in the River Clyde, and this has gone on deepening ever since. She had been my dream for years and to a man who hasn't pulled off too many of his dreams the achievement of this one, seventy solid feet of it, is a continuing joy. I even have a special identity I can slip into the moment I'm aboard, practically a boy again if I don't look in any mirrors. For all that radio telephone link I hadn't yet really corrupted my boat by doing any business from her, she remains my escape into the special sweetness of warm tropic seas, pure therapy for the apparently endless febrile pulsations of my affairs on land.

She has a crew of three, all Dyaks from Borneo, one more man than is really necessary, but they're a lazy, if bloodthirsty race, and you can't expect to work them hard. One is called the captain, but the other two don't have a marine rank or for that matter specific jobs, they're just around on an almost entirely automatic craft. There is no engineer, none needed for the twin sealed Gardiner engines serviced only occasionally by experts down in Singapore. Whenever possible I take the wheel myself. I also cook my own food.

If pushed, and in spite of her seine netter beam and timbering, the *Tanjong Pudu* can reach thirty knots, her diesels growling, but on this morning, and against a cross sea, I kept her to eighteen which was enough to send spray fountaining up from her starboard quarter. With only three hours' sleep I still felt that under this sky and in this light any kind of fatigue would be absurd. Coffee had woken me and bright day had done the rest.

Her wheelhouse windows were all open and wind blew straight through, brushing in passing the bare skin of my chest and back. Some seven miles to port was the coastline of Trengganu. For almost the whole length of the state this is marked by magnificent wide beaches which were now visible as a line of gold above the crumple of surf. I couldn't see them as detail but knew that palms marched down to the sand and sometimes out into it and behind this wind barrier were the casuarinas under which there is always a soft whispering. Villages were invisible, hidden back in shelter, and I had missed while still sleeping the only town of any size, the capital, Kuala Trengganu. Now we seemed to be moving in an area untouched by man, no sign of another ship, or a plane while the land looked as if it waited for discovery, rising up to the hump of the main spine under a covering of tufted jungle.

Malaysia's east coast feels much more remote than it is. Vietnam is only three hundred miles to the north and we were now practically on the route the big jets take from Singapore to Bangkok, but a sense of escape into a clean emptiness was real and I knew that I ran no risk of suddenly seeing a plastic detergent bottle tossed on a wave crest. It was a few years too soon for that.

I now had an island to steer by, Pulau Redang, a precipitous lump which looked as though it might once have been a volcano but had since been rubbed smooth and painted green. It appeared lifted above the sea, suspended by a hovercraft flap of blue-grey haze. I had once landed on Redang to find it a mini paradise peopled by a few Malays who fished and dried copra and were apparently all prepared to die young without bitterness from endemic malaria which no health service had yet dealt with. I remembered the long boats drawn up on sand, and nets drying, and palm thatched huts on stilts, and the horrible smell of tiny fish rotting in the sun on woven trays for the *blachang* paste essential to the really tasty curry. The island might be what I was looking for in the ultimate get away place, provided I took a ten-year supply of Ataprin with me and unless the project on which I was now embarked resulted in oil pollution from vast floating slicks that would kill the coloured fish and the sea birds. For the first time on my boat I was hit by a sense of sin, of being party to mass rape.

I gave the wheel to Busir, the captain, and went below to fry myself some eggs, standing with legs braced in the compact galley while the stove swung on its gimbals and I refused to allow myself to think. I took a plate through to the main cabin, raised a leaf on the fixed table, and sat down on the settee. I had a fork to my mouth when from up in the deckhouse came the electronic bleeping that is my phone bell. The circuit was open to allow the world to get at me. I climbed steps and plucked the handset from its recess.

'Paul Harris on board the *Tanjong Pudu*.'

'As simple as that,' Batim Salong said. 'I thought I'd try out the relay service. It seems to work very well. In some things we're quite contemporary.'

'And getting more so every day.'

'In a bad mood this morning?'

'I don't think I like phones on boats. Have you been kind to our Japanese connection?'

I hadn't stayed to see the meeting.

'I must say he is a most unobtrusive guest. He has practically become part of the furniture already.'

'The man's shy. He's not used to princes.'

'That should work to our advantage. Perhaps I'll continue to intimidate when he finally comes on the board of our company.'

'I wouldn't count on it. Batim, is this line safe?'

'Oh, very. I've made arrangements for that. You can call at all times with perfect confidence. Mr Akamoro and I will be expecting you to. And you'll be relieved to hear that Min has not as yet applied for any new concessions in this country.'

'That's something.'

'My dear man, it's an omen. Of our success. We have hit a favourable star.'

'Astrology is for boobs and actors. If there had been anything in that racket the oil companies would have had it all systematized years ago and saved themselves billions of dollars. We'll operate Kelatan Developments without a soothsayer.'

He laughed.

'Paul, why haven't you ever asked me for a cruise on your boat?'

'I didn't think we were that close. Besides, there isn't room for even a couple of your girls. I have a copra hold where most owners would have guest cabins.'

'I've never sailed off that coast. I've been looking at a map. Where are you now?'

I didn't have to glance at the chart.

'About eighteen north of Kuala Trengganu.'

'You've made good time.'

'My skipper held her to twenty through the dark.'

'And you drove fast to Kuantan, embarking at two-fifteen or thereabouts.'

'All right,' I said. 'Show off your intelligence service. Maybe we can put it to some use. What the hell have you done with it up to now? Or is it your procurer network?'

'I would remind you, Paul, that I am a prince of the blood.'

'We got past the kissing of hands some years ago, Your Excellency. Why do you have a man in Kuantan? The girls never seemed to me outstandingly pretty.'

'He's my cousin.'

'You have cousins in Kota Bharu, too?'

'Three.'

'Well, see they keep clear of me. I don't want my operation cluttered. And look, Batim, watch Akamoro. That gin palace you live in wasn't built for security.'

'In that you are wrong, my friend. It's as tight as a jail. The Japanese will not go for walks outside my walled garden. Keep in touch. When do you reach Kota Bharu?'

'Late this afternoon.'

'So we expect your first moves tomorrow?'

'Yes.'

'You'll phone a report in the evening?'

'If there's anything to tell you.'

'I've made arrangements for a security shut down on the use of a code word. You ring Seremban and say "Jawa". That puts the control into operation at once.'

'I'll remember.'

'Would you like to speak to the Japanese now?'

'No. I'd like to finish my breakfast.'

I made a call to my house in K. L. but radio relay wasn't so attentive to an ordinary number and it took a long time to get through. When I finally achieved this it was to a Chong sounding far away. I told him that I mightn't be home for a week, and that he was to exercise

Taro every day in the park. Chong had been on to the hospital and though his report on this wasn't too clear I gathered that Russell was still under sedation and apparently still unconscious, or near it.

When I got back to the eggs they had congealed on the plate. I scraped them into the sink disposal unit which would chop them fine and spit them into the sea.

The *Tanjong Pudu*'s aft hold is big enough to take a small car but we're not up to Jean Hyde's projected marine standards and don't have a power davit that could lift one out, so the only transport carried on board is a Honda. I don't like motor bikes but the machine was perfect for my needs in Kelantan. Aside from a good road running north-south along the main river and some tarred miles near the capital, communications over most of the rest of the state are still in the rutted track era, especially to the extreme south east. In that district the bridges are more gestures than weight bearers, some just palm trunks laid lengthwise and rarely replaced when rotted. Light trucks and Land-Rovers make use of fords and manage to get about but two wheels are better if you haven't a load. The only load I carried was a Colt .45 in a locked saddlebag.

My average speed was somewhere around seven miles an hour and though dust isn't normally much of a problem in a country where it rains every day and surface soil is red laterite my progress raised clouds on this track, as though I was travelling through an area of more recent geological formation still coated with a powdered pumice resistant to wet. At one stage I thought of stopping and hanging a handkerchief over nose and mouth but just carried on, trying not to breathe too deeply. Every now and then I stopped to dry out goggles. Flies were also a factor, the normal variety and a Malaysian variant on the western horsefly, but more aggressive and with a longer sting mechanism.

I was feeling that I'd allowed myself to become too romantic about this part of the world and certainly that pretence at a road could never be converted into a scenic highway. There had been the usual *kampongs* set amidst palms along the first part of my journey but for the last three-quarters of an hour nothing suggested man at all, no casual fields of tapioca or sweet potato, and absolutely no view, the track taking a line of least resistance along what looked like a dried-up water course. As far as I could make out I was travelling through a moderately elevated moorland, so arid that the jungle had never been able to claim it, the only tree growth some scrub stuff though there was plenty of the sword grass which only tigers and other big cats seem able to move through without getting chopped up. The area would appeal to snakes, lovely for pythons.

I'd kept the Honda's engine running the whole time even during stops and when I had to use my feet as reserve brakes but I reached a stream where the bridge had really gone, not even a couple of trunks left for a motor bike. The ford looked deep. I didn't want mechanical trouble so switched off the engine for a semi-carry.

At once I heard the popping of another motor bike. For a few seconds I thought it was a delayed echo, then there was revving for a slope. The sound was behind me, though I couldn't assess how far. The noise went on as I sloshed through water and was moderately loud by the time I was on dry ground again. I got into the saddle, kicked the starter and went roaring up a one in six gradient to a sharp right turn.

The climb continued beyond the bend, but with an easier slope. I didn't tackle this, getting off the still popping Honda to push it clear of the track into the shelter of rocks. I then used the throttle, cutting back, trying to suggest the sound of a bike moving into distance. The man behind me had certainly cut his engine at the ford, too. I heard it come on again, then the zoom up the gradient. I switched off, found my key-ring in a trouser pocket, unlocked the saddle bag and took out the Colt.

A second Honda came into view, but instead of zooming past towards the long slow hill the man on it stopped, put down both feet, then stared up towards where he had expected to see me. He was in a crash helmet, goggles, and had fitted the dust protection of a large bandana, as well screened as a bank robber. Quite slowly he turned his head, seeing me and the muzzle of a Colt. The range was ideal for a .45.

He appreciated this at once, sitting very still on the saddle, not trying to lift his hands from the steering bar.

'Enjoying yourself?' I asked in Malay.

He didn't seem to hear me.

'Cut that engine!'

The noise died away. There was the faintest whisper of a wind up here, and the whining of flies.

'You can use one hand to take that thing off your face.'

The hand came up. The handkerchief came down on his chest. I saw a black beard. He lifted goggles. It was Bahadur.

I swore at him in Cantonese. He might have been expecting this and was patient under it. When I'd finished he took off the crash helmet and long hair fell around his shoulders. He used the handkerchief to wipe his eyes. Then he took off the goggles and hung them on the handlebars, sitting with the helmet between his thighs. He stared up the track again.

'What do you think you're doing?'

'Following you.'

'Was that part of your assignment?'

'No, Mr Harris.'

'Get off that thing.'

He put the bike on its stand and came towards me, a white shirt as wet as mine. His greenish trousers were travel-stained. The normally clear whites of his eyes were bloodshot. He ignored the gun I was still holding up, sitting down on a hot rock, half-turning his back.

'Where did you pick me up, Bahadur?'

'Just south of Kota Bharu. I signalled, but too late, just as we passed.'

'So you just turned around and followed?'

'Yes.'

'I wasn't going too fast. I never do on these things. You didn't consider trying to catch up?'

'I was checking to see if you had a tail.'

'Thanks.'

He looked up.

'Well, you didn't see me!'

'You think I was being careless?'

'It looked like it.'

'Bahadur, I sat down for half an hour back there to eat a sandwich and drink a can of beer. What were you doing then?'

'Sitting down, too.'

'A hundred yards from me?'

'More than that. But I could see you. Have you a sandwich left? I haven't eaten for a long time.'

I went to my Honda, put the gun away and pulled out a plastic pack. Bahadur stared at the two slices of bread with corned beef between them, then took a big bite. He chewed as though my catering didn't give much pleasure.

'There's another can of beer if you'd like it?'

'No thanks.'

I sat on another rock. The man was very tired, but otherwise completely composed.

'Where did you spend last night?'

'About a quarter of a mile farther along this road.'

'Camping out?'

He nodded.

'Did you get any sleep?'

'Not much. And then about one there was a job for me to do. I went over to watch Min's operational team at work.'

He delivered that with a quiet triumph which reminded me of the way I had used Cantonese.

'I'm sorry I waved a gun at you, Bahadur.'

He swallowed, then grinned.

'I thought you held it pretty steady, Mr Harris.'

I lit a cheroot from a tin box.

'So you know where Min are?'

'Yes. About three miles from here. I can show you from the top of that hill. They're just back in the jungle, but not far. They've got a tent village. They're being supplied by helicopter.'

'*What?*'

'That's what woke me up. I'd finally got off to sleep.

It's a big one. And they may have more than one. One of those things that can carry heavy supplies. It seemed to be just food supplies last night, but in there they've got a forty-foot steel tower for a test drill.'

'How close did you get?'

'Close enough to count at least twenty men. There may be more.'

'No guards?'

'I didn't see any. Though I went carefully.'

'You mean they're just risking noise? Including 'copter din?'

'Yes. There's only the Klampa estate near them. No villages. And that machine didn't use much light coming in, nothing more than a quick flash on for landing. They took off again with no light at all, and there wasn't much moon last night.'

'Could you get any idea from engine noise where the 'copter headed after take off?'

'I think south-west.'

Bahadur rose, apparently restored by the sandwich.

'You'll get a better picture from up on the hill,' he said.

The top of the rise certainly offered a remarkable vista for Malaysia where jungle usually limits these. There was open country on a gentle slope right down to the sea some six or seven miles away. To the south there was massive forest, but this ended on an almost straight line, as though some change in soil chemistry had stopped the advance of hardwoods. We stood on a promontory above what was almost moorland, a big area suggesting Scotland except for that sword grass, and with something of the same sense of infinite space, a sky not muzzed by heat, but clear and high. Up here there was a breeze which discouraged the flies.

I spread out my map and checked it against the scene below, working back from the sea and a glitter of beaches to a sizable stretch of rubber. Klampa's commercial trees, dark green, made a neat rectangle that could have been a patch sewn on to cover a part grown threadbare. There were no other patches like it, no clumps of palms big enough to shelter a village.

We took off our shirts and spread them out to dry. Bahadur had done his job with a minimum of dashing about. He had come up the coast through Kuala Trengganu but the capital town had offered a complete blank, no hint of its use as any kind of base for a small expedition. He hadn't wasted time, simply travelled on to the concession site itself and then sat down to watch.

I thought of him working his way in the dark through sword grass to Min's camp site knowing that I wouldn't have liked the assignment. Beyond the vegetation-blasted helicopter pad was a path leading back into the trees, this unwatched even by a single sentry. Bahadur had probed around the encampment in which there had been a lot of activity even at that hour and it was his guess they were working a night and day shift system. Certainly the motor for working the probe drill had been clattering away and he came on pipes bringing water from a jungle stream for use under pressure. He had seen no sign at all of any European, but John Hyde could have been in one of the tents getting some sleep.

'You'd have to come by Klampa?'

Bahadur nodded.

'See anything?'

'Not much. The estate buildings are deep back in the rubber.'

'But they must know what's going on up in the jungle behind them?'

'Couldn't help it.'

'What about this track? Is it used much?'

'I never met anything on it at all, except a bullock cart nearer those villages just behind the highway. And while I was waiting here nothing passed in either direction. Of course it was night. But I think they must ship their latex out by sea. There's a small break in the beaches with an inlet deep enough for small boats.'

I could see that inlet as the eventual site for an oil harbour. The area was beginning to attract me again. The approaches to it weren't too pleasant but once on high ground you were in a kind of nirvana of isolation from the works of man, except for that rubber. It wasn't very aggressive rubber, either, showing few signs of a threatening expansion, no new plantings that I could see.

'What are you going to do, Mr Harris?'

'Go down to the estate.'

'What if Min have a man there?'

'Even if they do it shouldn't come to a shooting war. I suggest you get back to Kota Bharu and have a decent meal.'

'I'll stay. And watch through my glasses.'

I don't give orders that are obviously not going to be obeyed. He waited until I was on my bike and about to start the engine, then shouted:

'You should have the gun in your pocket.'

CHAPTER VIII

THE KLAMPA estate house and latex processing sheds had been built on a narrow strip between rubber and casuarina trees, an airless site permanently dipped in green gloom. I could see no quarters for hired labour at all, just those storage sheds and a one-storey building which looked as though it had started out as three rooms and then been added to on both sides, box after box. The homestead suggested a freight train parked in an unused siding and taken over by tramps who had added porches from scraps found on rubbish dumps.

A Chinese trade mark of teeming life was stamped everywhere, hens, dogs, pigs, geese and children, with any amount of washing hanging on lines that went back under rubber and could never get a hint of sun. Noise was human and animal. Half a dozen dogs charged me, but gave up just beyond kick range, and aside from this my approach to the kibbutz didn't seem to excite anyone. I wobbled round to what I assumed was the frontage and switched off.

I was quickly surrounded by about twenty children of assorted ages who all seemed friendly enough, but didn't press close. Then a shout from one of the porches dispersed them. Adults appeared, three young men advancing as a unit, with faces in unglazed windows behind them. The elders had no smiles for me. This seemed to be one of those frontier posts at which strangers aren't welcome, they didn't need outsiders to break the monotony, they bred their own new faces.

I got off the bike and pulled it up on its stand. One of the young men had stopped just slightly in advance of his companions, clearly the senior. You don't often see Chinese yellow down in the tropics where it is covered by tan but at Klampa they were screened from sun.

'What do you want?'

The Cantonese was clipped.

'I've come to see Mr Tan Ho Liew on business.'

'What business?'

'I'll discuss it with him.'

'He's not seeing anyone.'

Up on one of the porches I saw something flicker, and then again. It was a fan. Waving it was a seated figure totally obscuring his chair. From twenty feet away it might have been Russell up there brooding over me. I felt almost at home.

The sons didn't like it when I just started to walk towards their papa, and there was considerable yapping, but no attempt to run to physical interference. The fan went on flickering until I got to the foot of steps, then it stopped. I could see now that Mr Tan Ho Liew also had that complexion that could have come straight from North China.

I asked politely for permission to mount and this was granted. The sons didn't come up the steps with me. I stood over the patriarch but somehow I didn't feel tall, his authority was absolute in this green world and I don't think I've ever seen a man more sure of that. If Mr Tan had ever known stress that phase was long over and he waited through the final years of his living in the most agreeable way to do this, surrounded by a tribe to whom his word was law, sons, and sons' wives and grandchildren growing up remote from any influences likely to make them defect from the discipline. He was positively Old Testament, a senior citizen richly blessed by natural increase both in descendants and livestock. And if the day had to come when the economy of a small rubber estate couldn't produce enough food for all these mouths he wouldn't be around to see it.

I appeared to interest him. He shouted and an elderly woman brought out a light chair, following this almost at once with a tray of green tea and biscuits as though she always had these items ready for instant serving. I sat down and Mr Tan indicated that the traveller was to refresh himself. He then dismissed his sons, who went off looking surly. The tea might have been from Klang's own bushes, like everything else around here grown in shade. It had a sharp, bitter tang.

I was asked in surprisingly slow Cantonese what my business was and my spiel about this sounded even worse in Chinese than it would have done in English, a fairly literal translation of business efficiency guff, concerning the need for a centralized control in order to streamline production costs. I got held up, though, because I couldn't find the word for streamlining, which the Chinese don't go in for too much, and had to use my hands in smoothing gestures which intrigued the old man. The fan stopped moving.

I noticed that his eyes protruded, either from a slight thyroid condition, or surprise. I told him that the day of the isolated estate competing effectively with the large management overloaded combines was past, even though I knew this was nonsense and that in the rubber growing business the owner-producer tends to be twice as efficient as any hired overseer. Further, if you're running an estate as the head of a tribe you don't have to contend all the time with increasing wage costs, the work is done for love, or at least done, with a full rice bowl every day and bunch of firecrackers at the Chinese New Year as the reward for obedience and diligence. Mr Tan's set-up wasn't contemporary at all, and that's why he looked so happy. He left discontent to the next generation, as the wise man probably should.

I had prepared my material well enough, but I began

to feel an awful fool using it. Not one word of the jargon was getting over to the listener, or so it seemed, until he leaned forward and said:

'So you think there's tin under my trees, too?'

I took a deepish breath. The old man did not. He was off at a verbal gallop in sharp contrast to an earlier measured speech. He started to shout and there was a facial colour change, a rich, mottled purple spreading from his neck as lungs ran low on oxygen. I was the recipient of a pent-up fury that had been held for the right audience.

At first I wasn't able to pull much sense out of the performance, but then a picture began to emerge. Mr Tan was far from being a candidate for an asylum, just a picturesque reactionary of the kind who still survive in odd pockets even in our time and who want nothing more than a chance to set land mines under the trundling advance of alleged progress.

He had a few things to say about those fools up in the jungle with their flying trucks who believed there was tin beneath all this area. He didn't give a Cantonese damn if tin was packed in solid under the roots of his rubber, those trees were staying. If they liked they could churn up all the district for miles around with devil-conceived instruments brought in from the West but they wouldn't come one inch on to his land. Klampa was a rubber estate and it was going to stay a rubber estate. He had already been driven out of one property down south, selling for cash and emigrating to Kelantan for a bit of peace and quiet in which to conduct the good life and now the tin grabbers had followed him up here, too. Well, this time he wasn't moving for anything, or any money.

I was suddenly quite happy to let him roar on. Representatives of Min Kow Lin had certainly been here before me, and been booted out again. Driven to extremes, they might even have resorted to some of these exquisitely subtle threats which the Chinese keep for each other, and this had made Mr Tan madder than ever. Everything he valued in living had been affronted by some city type of his own race operating on the identical assumption that Hawakami had operated on with me, which is that all you have to do is assess a man's market value and then get out your cheque book.

The old man and I had a good deal in common, both still stinging from the insult of having been under-valued, though I had to admit that he was much more of a purist than I am. Sadly, it's the purists who get beaten in the end. Klampa rubber might stay for a while yet, with the estate surrounded by a new industrial complex and the noise of pumping engines, but erosion would soon begin to destroy this little world. Very shortly there would be jobs for the younger sons out beyond this green shade, together with Hondas and television. I couldn't believe that dedication to a father figure was going to keep the boys from taking those jobs, with the result that a cheap labour situation could be destroyed overnight and Klampa, as a viable economic proposition, would sag and then deflate. In fact the bell was already beginning to toll for Tan Ho Liew. I think he could hear it, which accounted for his anger.

I had a strong urge to tell the old man that what he should do was start sinking his own well immediately, straight through the roots of his trees, but remembered in time that I was a director of Kelantan Developments. The immediate threat to my company of Min Kow Lin's control of this estate had been removed and that was all I should be thinking about meantime. But I couldn't quite hold myself to the practical. I sat on a hard chair in the middle of a lost world with the hope that before Mr Tan had to admit defeat he'd be carried off, with dignity, by a stroke. From his colour now this seemed a very real possibility.

On the crest of the long hill up from Klampa I stopped the bike and looked back. Slanting afternoon sun was putting a spot down on a square of rubber, pointing it up. An oasis of man's effort in the wilderness was still under the blessing of remote peace, the sea beyond a placid glittering. Then, through a rustling of sword grass, I was sure I heard another sound, the chugging of a diesel power engine driving a probe drill.

I went on to look for Bahadur. Obviously he had pulled

132

his bike away from the track into a hide and was probably asleep somewhere under the shade of a rock. He was lying down all right, on his side, and motionless. His hands were strapped behind his back, his ankles tied together, and he was wearing a gag. The job had been done with a torn up fine cambric turban found in a Honda saddle bag. Binoculars with a broken strap were on the ground a few feet away.

The gag came off first, but Bahadur said nothing at all until he was free, he just kept spitting. Then he used a few words in Urdu.

'Were you knocked out?'

'Yes.'

'So you don't know when this happened?'

'I could still see your bike by the rubber estate. He chopped me. I didn't even hear him right behind.'

'So you've no idea what the man looked like? You didn't come round while he was trussing you up?'

'No. I came round as he came back.'

'What?'

'My bike. He took it. He was coming from Klampa. In a hurry. Minutes ago. Went past without stopping.'

He spat again, then looked up.

'Must have been on a bicycle. That's why I didn't hear anything, with the wind noise. I was using the glasses so I wouldn't see him top the rise.'

'Bahadur, could you have been spotted by a Min look-out?'

'How could he have got here in the time? That's a hard walk. It wasn't anyone from the camp.'

'Then a tail on us from Kota Bharu?'

'On a bicycle?'

'Why not? On this track I never hit speeds a cyclist couldn't have kept up with. At least if he had strong legs.'

'You were hitting fifty on the highway!'

'When the bicycle could have been in the back of a small van.'

'I was watching to see if we were followed.'

'You can't use a motor bike's mirror like a car's. There was a good deal of traffic. We'll go down to the Honda.

I'll open that beer. It's the only wet I've got. Can you walk?'

He stood by the motor bike massaging his neck.

'A karate expert,' I said. 'Maybe we'd better take it up.'

He used tepid beer as a gargle, spitting it out. This seemed to me to be carrying principle to ridiculous lengths.

'I'm going to the police about the Honda.'

'You're not, Bahadur.'

'It was practically new.'

'The firm will replace it. We're not attracting attention to ourselves at the moment. You'll have to ride pillion.'

He thought about that.

'It's best for you to be the passenger,' he said.

The *Tanjong Pudu* was tied up to a pole jetty in the Kelantan River, safely out of the main flow, tucked in against a grove of palms and only a few hundred yards from a thatched village. It was a perfect setting for the yacht marina that would be needed near the capital once the oil really started to flow. I hoped the planners would spare both the palms and the *kampong*. The little houses could easily be converted into an outdoor museum and craft centre with a shop offering wrought silver and gold thread sarongs at eight times their current prices. There was tourist potential in the area, dependent of course on some smart character, who could be Paul Harris, building a five-hundred-bedroom hotel with suites offering the cute gimmick of a second bathroom equipped with thunderbox and a planter's shower consisting of a stone jar of water and a dipper. I didn't think I'd have any trouble at all getting the finance if I was a big enough bastard to start it all up. Probably Batim Salong, now awake to commerce, would come in on the new deal, too, along with the City of London.

I infra-red-grilled an Angus fillet for dinner and sat down to eat it on a main cabin settee made softer by a pillow from my bunk for I was more than just saddle sore after the pillion ride behind Bahadur. My assistant was now established in the Kota Bharu hotel which was the best the town had to offer before the dawning of the Hilton era, once again in the role of a commercial traveller, and not in the best of tempers. He was equipped with one of three short-range two-way radios we carry on the boat and this meant that if the circuit on the master set in the wheelhouse was left open he could get in touch with me at any time he liked without having to go through phone relay.

I put two plates, a cup and saucer, a glass, and cutlery into the mini-dishwasher manufactured in Germany, switched on, then went up into the wheelhouse to call Batim. The code word Jawa certainly had its magic for I was through to him in under a minute, his voice straight from the sweet life that included recently a couple of brandies.

'Ah, my dear Paul, we were beginning to wonder if you were still alive.'

'I can hear you've been worrying.'

'Not me, actually, but the Japanese very much. He isn't with me at the moment so we can speak frankly. He prowls.'

'What?'

'Up and down my sitting-room, up and down my terrace, up and down the garden paths. Executive neurosis. It's very sad to watch. I'm beginning to wonder if it's catching. Most disturbing for a host. I ask you, where could he find a more beautiful setting in which to wait?'

I could think of a few places.

'Why don't you just stay in bed?'

'That's where I am now. Akamoro is worried about Klampa. He says it is the key to our project. Have you been there?'

'Yes. But I haven't turned the key.'

'You made an offer and it was refused?'

'No, I didn't make an offer. Min had been before me and got kicked out. Mr Tan is not accepting any offers at the moment. He hasn't begun to feel the pressures yet. He will, though it may take a little time. Meanwhile we can go ahead without worrying too much about the rubber estate.'

'Akamoro won't think that.'

'Tell him I'm handling this end in my own way. The important thing at the moment is that concession. How are you getting on with it?'

'I was in Kuala Lumpur today,' Batim announced, with pride. 'Things are moving in the right direction.'

I could see him reaching for a balloon glass that shouldn't have been part of the equipment in a Muslim household.

'Move them faster,' I suggested.

'There's someone knocking at my door. Just a moment.'

I was cut off by the heel of a hand over a mouthpiece and that lasted for all of two minutes. Then I got a worried voice it was easy to recognize.

'Mr Harris! This most bad news!'

'It's a hitch, that's all.'

'But surely, if you offer reasonable payment this man . . .?'

'No. At the moment Mr Tan is not selling.'

'It is most vital we secure Klampa estate at once!'

'What do you suggest I do? Apply a little terror? Hire thugs to burn down their rubber sheds?'

'You may offer what price you wish. I will authorize.'

'Money doesn't come into it. The owner wants to go on living under his rubber trees whatever happens around him. He thinks Min are after tin. We've found where they're working. They're not bothering too much about discretion. Supplied by helicopters.'

Batim was certainly right, just waiting had unnerved our colleague, and he wasn't really amenable to reason at all. I tried to calm him down and while at it moved with the phone held to one ear towards a locker where there was a bottle of whisky. I had to turn to reach this.

Air conditioning is often switched off in the wheelhouse but it was on tonight. It's expensive to run, and you learn to shut doors. The *Tanjong Pudu* was moored bow upstream which meant that it was the port sliding door we used to get to and from the jetty. The starboard door, on the river side, was open two inches. I hadn't gone out on to that deck this evening and all my crew were away in town on a pirates' hunt for women. I put the phone on the floor and a miniaturized shriek came from it as I was crossing the wheelhouse.

The man who had been crouched down below window level didn't consider trying to get across the boat to the jetty, he dived overboard. When a head broke through water that looked grey in misted moonlight it was at least thirty yards out, and in the full run of the current. I watched the man caught by that swirl and borne along by it. The flow was at least seven knots, too much even for a strong swimmer. He was in trouble.

Inside the wheelhouse Batim had taken over the shouting. I picked up the handset, put it back on its hooks, and cut the circuit. I got electric winches going, slackening bow and stern lines, then ran out to cast off from the deck. Back at controls again I brought twin diesels alive and in under a minute the *Tanjong Pudu* was grumbling out into the river. I used the hand-controlled spot, swinging it.

The swimmer had assessed his chances and wasn't trying to struggle against current, simply keeping afloat in it. It seemed probable that his idea was to save strength for use in clearing obstacles, rocks and flotsam, allowing himself to be carried along to that point where the force of river water was broken and dissipated by the sea's incoming tide. This meant at least a mile of dizzying travel, being spun in eddies and whirlpools.

I illumined the chart for the river. The navigable channel was deep enough, but tortuous and not always central to the stream's flow. I gave the boat power, putting her up to fourteen knots, much faster than I liked, but it brought me down past the swimmer at considerable speed and I cleared him by twenty yards, with the light swivelled around to pick him out as I went by. He didn't suggest a man in any kind of despair. I left him astern.

The chart showed a deepening to two fathoms across most of the flow and this stretch had a glassy surfacing with practically no eddies. I spun the wheel, pointing the bow towards the far bank, opening throttle. The boat spurted forward. I couldn't hope to keep position across current and had to bring her round again, half upstream, fighting to hold on three-quarters power. I locked the wheel, yanked a small scramble net from its locker and dropped this over the port side, where it hung from two clips fitting the low rail. Back in the wheelhouse I re-aligned the light to find that the man was going to be swept past the boat's stern. I reversed engines for twenty yards, then held again, this time fighting to keep the bow across current. A log hit the hull first, a noisy whack. The man's head swept through a lowered circle of light on the water, then out of it. I cut engines to keep twin props from functioning as a mincer if he missed a hold on rope mesh.

The *Tanjong Pudu*, without power, was being pushed broadside down the current, wallowing towards a turbulence that might be rocks or a sandbank, but I couldn't have engines on again without confirming that the man had a hold on the net.

The moon and reflected light from the boat's spot showed two arms out of the water and clawed hands dug into rope. A black head, face down, was pressed against the hull.

'Hang on. I'll get out of the current. Then I can help you.'

He must have heard, but didn't look up. One of his arms moved, as if to give fingers a stronger grip. From just above the inside wrist, and half-way to the elbow, was welted tissue standing out as a white line on brown muscle, a scar I'd seen before.

The man was too exhausted to get to the deck himself and I couldn't wait to haul him up. With engines on again, and hull shivering, the boat went hard astern towards water in the lee of a point beyond the *kampong*. I checked the chart for depth clearance. In five minutes we were in quiet water, engines idling.

There was no man hanging from the net. I went straight through the wheelhouse and out the starboard door. A head appeared. He had risked the reversed flow of the props while they were still turning, groping his way down under the *Tanjong Pudu*'s hull, but this had taken time and he had been forced to surface right in the lee of the boat. I could have hit him with a boathook and there was one lying along under the rail. As though he had thought of this he looked back, then used his legs to push himself from the boat's planking, swimming again.

I could see how tired he was. There wasn't much current here but even a side flow was almost too much for him. He seemed to be making for mangrove swamp five hundred yards downstream. If he got in amongst those tangled roots he was going to need a long rest before he was active again.

I put my boat full astern, brought her bows about, then made upstream for the jetty. It seemed to take a long time to get there and make fast. I then had to go down into the cabin for my Colt.

I ran up the jetty, into soft sandy soil under palms. Even before I was skirting the village a dog began to bark and other dogs took this up. A cock started to crow, its time clock malfunctioning, but no lights came on and there were no human noises.

In Kelantan mangrove fights the beaches, attempting a take-over, and here by the river, its roots fed by fresh water, it was thicker than usual and grew higher, a wall at the end of land. It offered a quaking uncertainty of mud on which the great plants stood with twisting tentacles probing down. Moonlight penetrated to a degree, quite bright on the channels that formed sluggish, briny tributaries to the river. There was a faint breeze and this set up a weird almost metallic creaking amongst branches. I listened for the sound a man might make in there, then moved in myself, using the octopus roots with care, testing footholds on their slippery writhings.

It was hot and the slime stank. I moved slowly to keep breathing quiet. I began to hear the smaller noises of the place, plops into water that could be rats disturbed. I watched for snakes, the curling vine that wasn't a vine.

Every few yards I stopped to listen, with hands on slubbery holds and black muck three feet down. If I fell into that stuff I'd survive all right, there is almost always solid bottoming after the ooze has taken you to about waist level, but mangrove is breeding ground for leeches and I have a horror of the things.

A brightness ahead turned out to be a clearing over a channel. When I reached this it looked man-made, almost a canal cut straight in from the river and wide enough for two boats to pass. It was filled with water and from a rising sea tide. At my side mud had been piled up on tentacle roots to form an almost solid embankment that offered a reasonable path. An exhausted man was going to take the line of least resistance through mangrove and I moved carefully down to meet him.

What looked like a huge log toppled down from the opposite bank but even before a heavy plop into water I knew what it was, and terror flipped up my heart beat. I faced the crocodile with my Colt lifted, seeing a snout and bulbous eyes, expecting every second the thrashing tail that meant action for attack. A slug from a revolver wasn't going to be much of a deterrent against that hide unless I waited until it opened its pink mouth on a climb towards me. I didn't feel like waiting.

The brute was a big one, old and experienced and perhaps not hungry. It reassessed the situation, decided it hadn't achieved the necessary surprise and turned up the canal, away from the river. In spite of what had seemed admirable self-control I was shaking like a man on the edge of a bad bout of dengue fever. I turned my head to watch a reptile's exit.

Breathing behind me failed to produce the right signal to my brain. I was about as unprepared for that chop at the base of my skull as a bullock for the humane killer.

CHAPTER IX

Busir, the *Tanjong Pudu*'s captain, hasn't much facial hair and only shaves about twice a month so that most of the time there are localized black patches spurting from upper lip and areas of chin. It was these I saw first, at close range.

I felt pain. The worst of it seemed to come from one foot, though there was a general aching of muscles and my head felt swollen. I moved an arm. Busir shouted something back towards the main cabin setting up unbearable vibrations inside my skull.

'Shut up!' I said.

He stood back from the berth, looking like a reproved child. I was in my own cabin for'ard, tucked up, with Busir as nurse. Light from the ports seemed horribly bright.

The captain had a flash of intuition and went away, to return with a bottle of whisky. I was assisted to a sitting position to sip my medicine and when asked what else I would like said chicken soup. It was an odd thing to order for breakfast but they managed to heat a can of the stuff and I had most of it.

It was ten in the morning and I had been found some nine hours earlier by three Dyaks coming back from town tanked up on *arak*. From what Busir admitted, rather sheepishly, it was pretty obvious that if I hadn't been laid out on the deck just beside the doors to the wheelhouse my crew wouldn't yet have missed me. This troubled them and they worked hard to be kind through their own hangovers.

A doctor had not been sent for, Dyaks don't use them much. What Busir had organized was a shore search which turned up clear evidence that I had been dragged, not carried, all the way from the edge of mangrove. One of my shoes had come off during this and they found it just beyond the village. The sharpest pain was from having no skin left at all on one heel.

The karate expert had brought me home, if roughly, when back there in the swamp he had immediately available one of the best fresh meat disposal units nature has yet evolved. The only possible conclusion from this was that my total elimination had not been scheduled, in fact it looked as though I was being carefully preserved for some reason. There was a certain comfort in this thought but at the same time I didn't like the way I had been towed back to the boat and just dumped.

'Sleep now, *Tuan*,' Busir said, stretching his English.

It seemed a sound idea. I slid down into the bunk and closed my eyes, for a few minutes hearing the noise made by my zealous crew as they thumped about, then losing that. When I came round again the light in the cabin had changed, mellowed from a sinking sun. Bahadur was sitting on the other bunk.

He looked worried. It could be that he felt it would be a bad blow to his prospects if anything happened to me at this stage in his career with Harris and Company.

'I thought I told you not to come to the boat?'

His head jerked up.

'It's all right, Mr Harris.'

'What do you mean, it's all right? We've got plenty of evidence that Min's tails are highly trained pros.'

'I wasn't followed.'

'You mean you didn't see anyone doing it. Did you walk here?'

'No. The Honda was returned to the hotel last night. I tried to get in touch with you on the radio.'

'How was your bike returned?'

'A waiter came up and said it had been left for me. He thought the man was Chinese but that's all he could say.'

'What time was this?'

'Quite late. About eleven. I must have been trying to get you on the set when you were lying on the deck. Your captain says they didn't get back until after one.'

'You didn't try to use the radio later?'

'I was on my bike. Going to Klampa.'

'Why?'

'To have another look at Min.'

'You found them still drilling?'

'No. I watched them moving out.'

'What?'

'Everything gone. That helicopter must have been at it all night. I didn't get there until after half-past three. I saw two flights. The last one was all personnel.'

'Are you saying they've taken everything? Even the drilling rig?'

'They didn't even leave one steel bar behind. I was all over their camp with a torch. There's nothing left but the site and a few holes in the ground. And now I know why, Mr Harris. The Tunku rang about an hour ago. I took the call. I said you weren't on the boat. He didn't want to give me the message but I think the Japanese told him it was all right. Min Kow Lin made formal application yesterday for the concession area. A party of them went along from their K. L. office, top brass, big stuff. They wanted to start open-cast tin-mining with rights over a twenty square mile area.'

I pulled myself up in the bunk.

'They were stalled?'

Bahadur grinned.

'It wasn't just a stall. It was a kick down the steps. They were told rights in the area had already been granted to another company. I think the Tunku would have told you a lot more than he told me, but he was pretty elated and I got quite a picture. It looks as though some very angry Chinese left the Ministry in under half an hour.'

I got the picture, too, and for a moment or two I could scarcely believe it. I had certainly been chivvying away at Batim about that concession but I hadn't really expected the thing to come through to us in much under three months, and with plenty of the usual red tape along the way. That he had been able to cut right through departmental procedures meant one of two things, he was a natural whizz kid, or certain persons in high places were still a little bit nervous of his potential if he ever should choose to move into the political arena. It certainly must have startled quite a few people to have a man everyone had thought retired from the world suddenly popping up again at the nerve centre, and at a time of general distress, too. I could imagine the relief when it was discovered that Batim's plans were to turn himself into a businessman, not a politician. The old boys' club had at once rallied around to support him in that role, delighted that it wasn't the other. Later, of course, they mightn't be so happy about

His Excellency, the chairman of Malaysia's first oil company, but before they got around to a new assessment we ought to have concession rights signed and Kelantan Developments a registered company.

'I expected more fight from Min,' Bahadur said.

'Not with the present tension, and after being kicked out like that. They've shown the big corporation approach; a project you've been working on has been effectively stymied by rivals. There's nothing you can do about that, at least not at the moment, so you cut your losses and pull out.'

'Then we've won?'

'I'll say yes with my fingers crossed.'

'There's something more, Mr Harris.'

'As good news, I hope?'

'I don't think so, though it may not be important. But it was why I was trying to get you on the radio last night. One of the bungalows at my hotel is occupied by a European woman. A Mrs Bruton. These places are at the end of the garden and you can't really see much of what's going on in them, but I did get a look at her. That blonde changes her name a lot. It's Mrs Hyde.'

I didn't ask him if he was sure; Bahadur's natural curiosity is going to prove a great company asset.

'The lady was joined this morning by a man with luggage. He signed in as Mr Bruton. He's on the short side and dark. Tough-looking. But I'd say he isn't very happy about life just now.'

'You had a good look at him, too?'

'Yes.'

'I wonder if he was depressed because he had just got the sack from Min Kow Lin?'

'Could be,' Bahadur said.

'I think you'd better get back to your hotel. Keep an eye on the Hydes. If they make a move let me know.'

Bahadur was looking quite cheerful, as though my sufferings had done him a lot of good. When he had gone I had a slice of bread and butter and a glass of powdered milk, then phoned Batim.

The Tunku *was* elated. He was already seeing himself

in his life's role, achieved belatedly perhaps, but in which he was still going to be a big thing. He didn't actually brag to me but a certain smugness travelled over the airwaves and he came very near to issuing an order that I was to return to K. L. at once, presumably to celebrate. I had to remind him of the Klampa estate factor, as yet unsettled.

'We will squeeze the Chink out, Paul!'

'That may take time. And during it a well could be sunk from his property.'

'Does he know it's oil?'

'No, he thinks it's tin. But Min could tell him. And if they're as angry as I think, the idea of doing that might appeal to them, along with an offer to finance his rig.'

That silenced Batim for a moment, then he said:

'I think Mr Akamoro wants to talk to you.'

I waited again.

'Mr Harris, I am listening on extension.'

'Well, it's a common practice.'

'We must secure Klampa estate!'

'That's why I'm staying up here. I'll have another try tomorrow. This time I'm going for an option on his mineral rights, with the proviso that we don't attempt to exploit them without his permission. He might just play on that. After all, it would be money for nothing and no risk to his trees. And it would cover our flank.'

'This good idea, Mr Harris. Please put into effect immediately.'

'Well, I'm not going down there today. It would mean coming back in the dark over a very bad track and though Min's camp has gone I've got a feeling they've been a bit careless about contacting their fringe operators. To call them off.'

'I don't understand?'

'While they were clearing that camp down south I was attacked up here.'

'Oh! Again?'

'Same man, too.'

There was a hissing of sucked-in breath from a country estate near Seremban.

'You are not careful enough, Mr Harris. You are hurt?'

'Bruised as before. I was knocked out, but I think went into sleep from unconsciousness, otherwise I wouldn't be feeling as well now as I am.'

'You must watch all the time!'

'With Min out of the picture now surely not?'

'One cannot be sure. You must run no risk.'

It was nice to know that though Batim thought he could now run Kelantan Developments without me, Akamoro didn't.

The Malaysian sunset is nearly always worth watching if you have the time. Some people make a fetish of it and that ritual of pouring the first hard drink while the flaming dies is still continued by a few reactionaries of whom I am not one. What I did do was take a malt out on to the *Tanjong Pudu*'s hatch cover for that first coolness before the mosquitoes get active which is why I saw a car stop at the edge of palm trees. The woman who walked from it towards the boat was a blonde.

Jean Hyde was wearing a dress again, this time not a midi, but a cotton print which offered a lot of thigh. She walked as though conscious of an audience, just slightly swinging a white handbag almost as though it was that basket of flowers with which leading ladies tend to make their entrances in operetta. The mood was clearly carefree, perhaps a bit too heavily defined as such, and it made a malt drinker on a hatch cover wonder what he should be bracing himself for.

I stood. She managed the single plank herself before I reached the boat end of it.

'Hello, Paul. Surprised to see me?'

'No.'

'You have a snooper out?'

'Yes.'

'An Indian with a black beard? I thought I recognized him. Wasn't he with you at the hotel?'

'That's right.'

'Tell him he hasn't the first idea how to tail a woman.'

'I'll do that.'

'Aren't you offering me a drink? What's that you're having?'

I told her. She said she would have it straight from the bottle without water and I went into the wheelhouse for a glass. When I came out again she was walking around narrow decking inspecting my boat, and with a knowledgeable eye. I gave her a double 103% proof and waited for the coughing to start, but it didn't. She took a second sip and rolled this around her tongue before swallowing.

'I suppose you own the distillery?'

'If I did do you think I'd be living in Malaysia?'

'It's lovely stuff.'

I offered to get a chair but she preferred the hatch. She didn't exactly lie back on it but there was still a great deal of thigh exposed. We discussed boats for a while, a shared enthusiasm, and while we were at it the sky went psychedelic, imposing strange colours on the land, the *Tanjong Pudu* and us, a discotheque frenzy through which her eyes kept their own remarkable tone. She said suddenly :

'You know John's here, of course? And you've guessed he got the sack?'

'It seemed probable.'

'He blames me. They all do. That bloody Chink company. There have been hot words over radio links. Was I really the leak to you?'

'You made me curious.'

She thought about that for a moment.

'I hate John having this on me,' she said. 'It's a bitch thing for him to have on me.'

'You've nothing on him?'

'Plenty. But I can't serve it now. It isn't fresh.'

There had been a happy reunion in a Kota Bharu hotel bungalow.

'You won't believe me, of course, but I didn't like doing what I had to.'

'In the circumstances it was a moral obligation?'

'Let's skip the sarcasm, shall we? It was an obligation.'

'To help with a kidnapping? Two of them?'

'They weren't going to hurt you or the Jap.'

147

'You draw the line at being accessory to murder?'

She looked at me.

'Yes. But we had a real stake in this thing.'

'So much per barrel?'

'No. We didn't rate a percentage. Min wouldn't play on that. But John was to be managing director of their new subsidiary. He was to set it all up. He'd have pulled it off, too, but for me. That's going to burn between us. The trouble is I can't shake this feeling I've been a damn fool. It hurts.'

I sat down beside a suffering girl. Our previous contacts hadn't brought us very close. This one was beginning to. I was conscious of those thighs. I leaned forward, holding my glass in both hands. One of her hands came up and travelled over the back of my shirt to the area of karate chop bruising.

'Take me down to your cabin, Paul.'

'I don't think so.'

'I'm not your line?'

'What are you offering? Reparations?'

'Sort of. Not tempted?'

'I have a sensitive neck.'

She laughed.

'You think you know everything, Paul. But you don't. Not until you've had me. Give me some more of that nectar.'

I reached for the bottle and poured.

'I see you kept your taxi waiting,' I said.

'It can wait. And wait.'

'I knew a man once who used to take a taxi to the golf course and keep it waiting while he played eighteen holes. He's bankrupt now.'

Her eyes were wide. She said, very softly:

'Better than golf, Paul. Much better than golf.'

'You want me to take your husband on?'

She nodded.

'And why should I?'

'For what goes with it.'

'What would John say about that?'

148

'Nothing. Believe me, nothing. And think of the time we'd have.'

'When?'

'While he was on field trips. There'd be lots of field trips, wouldn't there? Have you got a woman now?'

'What the hell business is it of yours?'

'A girl likes to know about the opposition. I'm a fair competitor. I just wipe it out.'

She was smiling.

'I'm sorry,' I said, 'but I'm not employing your husband. He's probably a top geologist but you don't pass our company test for executives' wives.'

For just a moment she sat quite still, then she got up.

'I told the silly bugger it wouldn't do any good.'

There was no venom in that. The girl had a kind of honesty, if not of a very endearing variety. She walked carefully up the plank and on to the jetty, then down along uneven poles, never wobbling and not looking back. I wasn't expecting any further signals between us but half-way along a sandy track to the car she stopped and turned, lifting a hand to wave. I didn't know whether to laugh or not. I lifted a hand, too.

Up in the bows I saw Busir's head and shoulders pushed through the fo'c'sle hatch. He was staring after a desirable woman, tugging at hairs on his chin as he did it. There was a crackling on the open radio circuit, followed by a voice. I went into the wheelhouse.

'Bahadur calling *Tanjong Pudu*. Over.'

'Hello,' I said.

'Mr Harris! The Hyde wife left the hotel. I followed her but she went into a shop. She must have got out the back way.'

'She's been drinking with me. She says you don't know the first thing about tailing a girl. But don't worry about it. Have your supper now and get a good night's sleep.'

The hospital in Kuala Lumpur put me through to the matron for a little chat. I had met her once. She was no starched relic from the days of iron discipline, but the new thing, slightly plump, fashion conscious, and eking out

149

her reign as probably the last European in her office by an absolutely undentable sweetness to everyone. She was sweet to me, explaining how terribly happy they all were about the wonderful progress Russell had made against great odds. Those odds, of course, were the fact that he had been delivered to them more or less as a bag of dissolution and modern surgery plus the best of nursing techniques had staged another triumph and looked like turning out my partner as two-thirds of a new man. It was all up to Russell himself now. If he took reasonable care and no booze it might well be that his best years lay ahead, those golden days of late autumn mellowed by philosophy.

I was then switched over to a private room. I sent my voice over the air slightly louder than necessary as we tend to do when uneasy.

'Hello! Is that you, Russell?'

'It is.'

I took a deep breath.

'How are you?'

'Just in from a brisk run around the *padang*.'

I laughed. Russell just waited.

'Matron says you're getting on wonderfully,' I told him.

'Does she? They took out one drainage tube yesterday but I've still got two left in.'

I tried to strike the right note.

'That's getting rid of the beer.'

He had no comment.

'How are you feeling?'

'Like a man who's lost twenty pounds too quick. They weighed me this morning. Where the hell have you been? Chong was here. He said you'd gone off somewhere and left no forwarding address. He thought you were on your boat?'

'I am. A thing blew up. One of our junks in trouble in Singora. Seeing it was a mix up with the Thais I thought I'd better straighten it out myself.'

'What sort of thing?'

'The captain was jailed. But it's not important, Russell. You're not to worry about anything.'

'I have nothing to do but lie here and worry. Are you

phoning from Singora? If you are it's a helluva clear line from across the frontier.'

'It's radio relay, from my boat. At Kota Bharu. We stopped in here on our way down the coast.'

'What for?'

'Well, we had a rough passage and I wanted a good night's sleep.'

'You're a liar. You've never been near Singora at all. You're on to Min oil, that's what you're doing. What made you go to Kelantan?'

'Russell, I'm on my way home and we'll have a talk just as soon as I get there.'

'I've got a feeling that Japanese is mixed up in this. Is he with you?'

'Certainly not. Now will you stop the interrogation? I'm not going to talk any more about this over a radio link.'

'So you *are* up to something? You think you know where the oil is?'

'I don't think anything of the sort.'

'Which means you *know*.'

'Russell, I'm hanging up now. Matron says you tire easily.'

'I'm warning you, Paul. I said it before and I'll say it again, if you set yourself up against Min I'm out. I want a quiet life after what I've been through.'

'You'll get it. Surrounded by loving care.'

'Who from?'

'Remember what you said about wanting a son?'

'That was when I thought I was dying. Did you go to see Batim Salong?'

'I'll tell you all about it as soon as we meet.'

'If I have a relapse it's on your head. I want you to ring me here the moment you get back to K. L. Get that? It doesn't matter what time of day or night it is. I don't sleep much. I've made them put calls straight through to me.'

'I'll do that, I promise.'

I was sweating when I hung up.

The *Tanjong Pudu* has double planking, which means that

a man walking on her deck can't be heard in the cabin below unless he is wearing heavy boots. I'd gone to bed feeling reasonably secure behind shatterproof glass and mortice locks, my sleep natural and unvisited by the kind of nightmare which brings you clawing back to wakefulness. The forward cabin shares a bulkhead with the crew's quarters but deafening had been one of the overheads in the building of this boat and I could hear nothing at all from the fo'c'sle, so it must have been intuition which had me wide awake and sitting up. The illumined dial of my watch said five fifty-three which meant dawn was near, though the sealed ports were still dark. I was tempted to lie down again and continue with my Kelantan holiday, but instead pushed myself out of the berth and groped through the main cabin to the wheelhouse steps.

To starboard the river ran dark and to port I could just see where the end of the jetty merged with a fringe of palms. In minutes there would be the first grey light. I went out on deck.

A new day nearly always comes sweetly in the tropics, making all kinds of promises likely to be cancelled later, but in that first hour you can believe almost anything; that the black panthers have given up dog hunting and gone vegetarian and a ritual circling of carrion birds a hundred feet above the jungle roof is nothing more than morning setting up exercises. There is the feeling that the world has been given a new start during the night as the direct result of a high level Providence conference. But now I couldn't get on that upbeat beam, a kind of aching in spiritual bones said there were bad times ahead.

I stared at shadow under the palms but nothing moved in it. The village offered no lights and the sound of the river covered all other sound. I was turning into the wheelhouse again when I noticed something white on the deck just at the foot of the plank to the jetty. It was a piece of paper, folded, and weighted with a stone. The note was in English, printed with a blunt pencil in block capitals.

'PLEASE TO COME QUICK KLAMPA.'

There was no signature. I thought about a lure to

get me on that lonely twisting back track, but dismissed the idea, the message had a kind of simple honesty from stress. I shouted for Busir to get the Honda out of the hold and then went below for coffee.

It was after ten when I reached the high ground overlooking a future oil field, and I stopped for a moment or two to wipe dust off my face. I had hit speeds on that trail which would have impressed Bahadur and worn the composition sole of the shoe on my undamaged foot using this as a drag break. The slope to the sea looked tranquil enough, nothing stirring on a road I could see all the way to the patch of rubber.

There were no immediate signs of anything wrong back in Klampa's permanent shade either, the residential train still there and it was only when I was quite close to this that I realized something was missing beyond. The long sheds used for storing the latex had gone. Where they had been were some charred uprights. What looked like steam rose from ashes.

On an estate as remote as this one those sheds could have been holding anything up to a year's take of raw rubber, the half-processed sheets stacked waiting for transport to market. It was improbable that old Tan had gone in for industrial risk insurance.

I cut the engine. Dogs were barking somewhere, but shut away, for they didn't come running. Pigs were out of sight and the hens seemed to have taken to the rubber. The silence was ominous.

The Chinese have regular disaster as part of their race history and the usual reaction to it is to get back to work at once. No one was getting back to work here. One man came out of the boxes, but slowly, as though just able to drag himself from a sleep of utter exhaustion. There were buckets lying on the packed earth between him and me, just dropped when the home fire brigade had seen there was nothing more to be done.

The eldest son walked with his arms straight down at his sides. He stopped a few feet from me, as though he didn't want to walk any farther than he had to. He looked past me towards the casuarinas.

'When did this happen?'

'In the night.'

'Anyone hurt?'

'No.'

'Did you write me that note?'

He nodded.

'Does that mean you connect me with this in some way?'

He didn't say anything.

We had no audience, not a single face at those windows with storm shutters propped up from them on poles. I didn't ask if they had any idea how the fire had started. It's easy enough to get a latex blaze going, an arsonist would only have to leave a bundle of oiled rags alight and then clear off. And a fire was a simple way to break down a stubborn old man's resistance to change. I didn't have to look about me again to know that Klampa was being run on a shoestring. It simply wouldn't have the reserves to stand up to a year's production loss.

'Please come to my father,' the eldest son said, with grim politeness and still not looking at me.

We went towards that verandah on which I had been entertained and up the steps, into the room beyond which was so dark it took a moment for my eyes to adjust. The patriarch was in a bed set just behind one of the windows, with pale, tree-stained light across his face. He stared at me for what seemed a long time, then said in English:

'I sell now.'

Batim Salong was equipped with the standard rich man's defence pack against intrusions from outside his special orbit, very little imagination. There were two kinds of people in the world, his minority grouping and the rest. It wasn't going to be easy to drive a prince down a more humanitarian road in the matter of oil revenues. He made about as likely a candidate for his future role of champion of the people as a Greek shipping magnate. His genes had given him charm, wit, sex appeal, pride and a high IQ but not a droplet of compassion that I'd noticed. I found I was liking him less this afternoon and he was revising his feelings for me, too, almost at screaming pitch.

'All right, Batim, all right! I accept that you didn't get on to your cousins up here.'

'You think I do such a petty thing through my relations?'

'It's not petty to the Tans.'

'Look, why do you go on telling me about the troubles of these Chinese? They get money if we buy the place, don't they? I don't see why I have to hear about some sheds burning down. Why couldn't it have been an accident?'

'A very convenient accident for us now that Min's out of the picture. The Tans think we did it. I've just come from preliminary discussions about price with a family who never once looked at me while it was going on. They had decided it was policy to conceal hate but didn't trust their eyes to go along with policy.'

'How terrible for you, Paul. You'll have me weeping soon.'

'I doubt it.'

'My God, you still think I had something to do with that fire, don't you?'

'No.'

'I demand an apology!'

'All right. I apologize.'

'That's not good enough. I don't accept it. I'll resign from the company.'

'In that case so will I, Batim. With a full statement to the press as to my reasons. These will be that I don't think a Japanese financed company with local front men is likely to serve Malaysia's best interests in the matter of newly discovered oil. That ought to cause a pretty stink in a time of political crisis.'

'So now you're using blackmail, too, eh?'

'I don't mind at all using it against the powerful. Let's stop shouting at each other. I think it's time for a cooling off period.'

'I could blow you sky high with Akamoro and Hawakami.'

'Of course. The whole thing's over if you and I lose confidence in each other. Akamoro isn't by any chance listening on an extension?'

'He's in the swimming-pool.'

'Good place to be on a hot afternoon. Try it yourself.'

I hung up and switched off relay to keep him from a come back, then went out on the deck to stare at the river.

Who the hell else was there in the country who wanted Kelantan Developments to become big? Bahadur? I didn't think my assistant would carry personal initiative to the lengths of arson. The intelligent man with a legal training rarely resorts to a criminal act to further his own interests, there are too many other tricks available to him that are nicely within the law. This seemed to leave just one alternative which was that the man with the scar on his arm had not, after all, been working for Min. My head hurt. I didn't want to think about who he could have been working for, but I had to.

Down in Singapore there is a policeman who has shown a sharp professional interest in my activities on a number of occasions, though this hasn't in any way marred the happy relationship between us. Since the split between the island and the mainland we haven't seen so much of each other, though we both make a point of keeping in touch whenever possible.

I put through a call to his office. This had to cross a frontier which is sometimes subject to tensions and I seemed to have struck one of the days for the connection took nearly half an hour. After that I had to be screened by his two secretaries.

'Kang, here. Well, Harris? If you're in Singapore you can take me out to dinner tonight. There's a new restaurant that's much talked about but no policeman can afford. Our salaries are always twenty per cent behind inflation. Shall we say seven-thirty at the bar of the Hilton? You can save whatever little problem you have till then, I'm busy.'

'I can't make dinner. I'm tied up in the Kelantan River.'

'On that boat? It'll be sabotaged one day and you'll be blown up with it, mourned by us all. Though it'll not be any responsibility of mine, thank God. Why are you disturbing the peace of the Kelantanese?'

I decided to switch him from that tack.

'You'll be sorry to hear that Russell has been very ill.'

'Oh? Well, we all have to go sometime. He's had a long run.'

The superintendent had distress under firm control. I knew that despite their fairly close contact at one period the two men didn't waste much affection on each other.

'Is it the beer at last?' Kang asked politely.

'Indirectly. But he appears to be recovering. I rang to ask if you'd do something for me.'

'No.'

'A matter of your records. Identification.'

'Nationality?'

'Chinese.'

'We have a million and a quarter of them, including me.'

'How many knife fighters?'

'About twenty thousand.'

'This man has one of those things you policemen love so much. A real scar. He also looks like a Manchu.'

'Listen to the ethnologist.'

'You know damn well what I mean, Kang. Not a south China type.'

'Is that what you label me? The clearly marked coolie ancestry?'

'Yes.'

'You get no service from the Force down here.'

'The scar is on the inside of his left arm, from wrist half-way to elbow. The wound was so deep it's a wonder the hand wasn't paralyzed. He must have had good medical treatment and therapy. A man of some importance, I'd say, though subject to discipline beyond his own inclinations. No ordinary thug. Also a karate expert, and I mean expert, not one of those gymnasium amateurs.'

'Chopped you, has he?'

'I'm still recovering.'

'*Mister* Harris, I must point out that this is entirely outwith our jurisdiction and authority. I was against the big split between our two countries, but it has its compensations. I'm rarely called on to investigate you these days. I've got a strong feeling suddenly that if I give you any help at all it could result in an international incident. Go to the local police in Kota Bharu.'

'Remember the dinner I'm buying you soon.'

'Also, I deeply resent the suggestion that all really well-trained criminals in South East Asia originate in Singapore. In fact only ninety-seven per cent of them do. Describe this man's face. And I don't want any hint of racial discrimination in the way you go about that.'

'His face is almost Mongolian, very much on the round side. He has about as much expression as a grapefruit.'

'Voice?'

'I've never heard him speak.'

'How often have you encountered him?'

'Twice. Both times he won.'

Kang was silent for a moment, then he said:

'You know, my friend, you're not a boy any more.'

'That comes home to me quite often. Though I was propositioned by a blonde yesterday.'

'In Kelantan?'

'Yes.'

'The state must have changed since I knew it. There were no blondes then. What did she want, I mean aside from you?'

'A lot, actually. Kang, will you get on to records for me?'

'Yes. But I'm not calling you via relay on that boat. You can ring me. About seven. Don't make it much after that, I have a home to go to since it is not going to be a night on the town.'

I was sitting in a wicker chair in the cool of a sealed wheelhouse staring up at the pole jetty when Bahadur came out on to it riding his Honda, with what seemed all of his gear strapped on the back. He pulled his transport up on its stand and then came down the plank looking serious. A door slid open and shut again.

'You look ready for travel,' I said.

'I am. The Hydes left on the three-thirty train for the south. I've moved out of the hotel. It's not first class. I was bitten by bugs last night. I'm welts all over. When do we sail?'

'When the crew wakes up, which could be any time now. But you're not coming with us.'

'Yes I am. I've always wanted a trip on this.'

158

Sikhs aren't normally nautically minded.

'I have a job for you to do which I'd hate to have to do myself. I know that isn't the principle of leadership.'

'No, it isn't,' Bahadur said.

'You're going to stay in Kelantan until you've completed the purchase of Klampa estate. It's a chance for you to use your legal training. But if you have to bring in a local lawyer I don't mind.'

'What makes you think I can buy that place?'

'They're waiting for you. It's fixed. I was down there again.'

I told him about it. Nothing changed in his eyes. His race are rarely moved by the sufferings of Chinese. He would be a cold bargainer and I didn't want this.

'I was going to offer them sixty thousand Malay dollars,' I said.

'What? Those trees will be out of production in ten years. I didn't see any new plantings.'

'Nevertheless you will make it seventy thousand.'

'Mr Harris, that's crazy!'

'Hawakami is paying.'

'I don't care who's paying, it's the principle of the thing. It's a ridiculous price.'

'Bahadur, we're moving a tribe to make it more convenient for us to get oil. You will not haggle. They're under shock. This is no time for a slick performance. Get the papers signed as soon as possible. When everything is tied up ring Seremban and ask for Jawa. That will reach Akamoro. You'll find him twitching for your good news.'

'The way things move up here I could be stuck for weeks!'

'You can spend what you like. Get yourself bug free accommodation.'

'What's the good of being able to spend what I like in Kota Bharu?'

Busir came down the deck from the fo'c'sle followed by his two deckhands.

'We're about to cast off,' I said. 'Visitors ashore.'

CHAPTER X

THE RADIO weather reports were somewhat nerve-tightening. The area towards which we were travelling was promising Force Eleven before morning, and Eleven is a great deal of wind. Already it was gusting Seven to Eight, the gale coming at us out of the north from the direction of Cape Camau in Vietnam. The *Tanjong Pudu* rode cross seas in a manner that would have brought joy to her builder's heart though in the wheelhouse we were beginning to feel the motion somewhat, and if you moved anywhere it had to be from handhold to handhold. I didn't think Bahadur would have enjoyed this cruise too much.

After dark I had cut speed to under ten knots and for some time now had been thinking that maybe this wasn't the night on which to test my boat's typhoon resistance qualities or my seamanship. The Kelantan experiences had been tiring and I still had a lot on my mind. If there had been a good port handy I'd have run for it, but there wasn't, just Kuala Trengganu offering a river mouth anchorage that was safe enough even from a northerly but only after you had negotiated sand bars marked treacherous on the chart, which means that nobody really knows where the hell they are. I considered trying to run in there in the pitch dark through pounding surf and then put that idea firmly to one side. The thing to do was keep deep water under our keel and carry on towards Kuantan through a howling turbulence.

The moon wasn't going to help us at all, the only thing visible beyond windows polished by wipers were the tips of increasingly outsize waves. We went up water hills and sank into their valleys. My job was to see that we took those ascents at the right angles to prevent a crest from smashing down on us, and though our decks streamed all the time I managed this not too badly. The boat creaked in this test of her timber frame and hull and every now and then her props came out which shook us up a bit, but aside from the loss of some unsecured crockery in the galley everything was tight enough. Once I recovered from the initial tension I began to half enjoy the storm, and I had an audience to watch my performance at the wheel, all my crew in the deckhouse with me.

It was almost a party. Dyaks have generations of voyaging in open boats behind them and a bit of weather tends to stir them out of a normal lethargy into near manic excitement. The three behind me had absolutely nothing to do on an automated craft except watch. They chain-smoked, told dirty stories, and went off into roars of laughter.

It was seven-forty-seven when I remembered about a call to Kang.

'Busir, take over.'

He was delighted to do this. Half a minute after the wheel came under his hands we shipped the top quarter of a sea over our bows and I was flung across the deck from the control panel to be smacked into our fire equipment locker.

'Don't be so bloody slap happy!' I yelled, in English.

'Okay, *Tuan*. Mistake.'

Their philosophy is that you can have a round dozen of mistakes before the one that is going to get you hits. And only a couple of generations back these people had believed that every self-respecting male died young, either in battle or fighting the sea.

'When I say seven I mean seven,' Kang said from Singapore. 'If I hadn't been held up you'd have been out of luck. What's that noise?'

'A typhoon brewing.'

'You're in it?'

'And moving towards the epicentre.'

There was a burst of static.

'I can't hear you, Kang.'

'I asked how you were standing up?'

'We're not, we're hanging on.'

Busir laughed. He knows far more English than he admits.

'Records have surprised me again, Paul. They've come

up with a man who could fit your moon face Manchu. There's even a photograph of the scar. Pity I can't send you a radio picture.'

'I'm not having any more gadgets on this boat. Who is he?'

'Name of Hsien Ho. I'd say we can be seventy per cent certain. Perhaps more than that.'

'Which means you're sure. Let's hear about him quick. I think static is going to cut us off.'

'Not quite a Manchu but near enough. Comes from a town just south of the Great Wall . . . Sifengkow. That is, he was born there. Left at the age of three, with his parents. They immigrated as a family to relations down here. The father was . . .'

Kang's voice faded. I shouted.

'Come in louder! What was the father?'

'A butcher. In a way the son has carried on the family tradition, with knives. He's been through our hands three times, twice for inciting a riot, once for assault with weapon for which he got three months. Last time we had him in was over the kidnapping of Li Shui, the ointment tycoon. That was three years ago. The kidnapping charge wouldn't stick and we had to let him go. There are at least two sudden deaths we treated as murder which had tiny little red arrows from them pointing towards Hsien. I worked on one of the cases for nearly two months and all I got out of it was those little red arrows up in my head.'

'You watch him?'

There were noises that could have been more static or Kang erupting.

'You ought to know enough about our situation not to ask a damn fool question like that. No, we do not watch him. To watch fringe characters like Hsien effectively we'd need at least another five thousand men on the Force. There are occasional checks, that's all. The last one came up with the fact that he'd been out of Singapore for some time. Believed in Malaysia.'

'Political orientation?'

'Can't you guess? There's not much doubt he's an operative for the Malaysia Peoples' Liberation Front. As you

162

know that's totally non-political except that all its literature and most of its finance comes from Peking. Which could well account for Hsien's being up your way in a time of rioting. Organizing Chinese resistance to Malay aggression.'

'Who's showing bias now?' I shouted.

'I'm just using the jargon, friend.'

'You think this Hsien is a big man?'

'I'd say top echelon or very near it. An activist on occasion himself for special jobs, but basically admin. Which makes his lowly function as a tail on you interesting. If I were you I wouldn't like that.'

'I don't.'

'Take good advice. Watch it. And though it goes against my initial British training to say this, wear a gun. Got one?'

'A Luger. Hsien got my Colt. If it was Hsien.'

'Assume that it was. Have you done anything special to annoy Peking recently?'

'No.'

'Or the local Reds?'

'I don't think so.'

'Of course, your mere presence in Malaysia is an offence.'

'Thanks.'

'I'd miss you. You buy a hungry policeman meals. It's the only corruption I allow myself.'

The *Tanjong Pudu* went into a trough stern first, and wallowing. A wave coming up from port didn't lift her again, it broke. We were buried in water. I travelled towards the back of the wheelhouse, the handset coming with me to the end of its cord, then ripped from my fingers. Two unemployed crewmen and I made something of a heap on the deck. Above a great roaring and crackles on the phone line I heard Kang's thin shout:

'That sounded bad. They tell me drowning's a clean death.'

Something just over two hundred miles took us twenty-five hours aboard the *Tanjong Pudu*. The trip was one of those little voyages likely to put a boat owner off cruising for quite some time. Before it was even half over the thrill of a contest with the elements had quite gone and I climbed into the Zodiac at Kuantan feeling like a man who has lost something important from his living, it could be my love of the sea. Another two hundred miles by road should have topped off exhaustion, but somehow it didn't, to have four well sprung wheels on a hard surface did a lot to restore my morale.

It had been dark for some time when I reached Kuala Lumpur. I put the Ford in the garage and walked towards a house that offered no welcoming lights, not even a glow from the hall. I went up steps, used my key, found switches and shouted for the dog. Taro didn't come.

After what seemed a long time Chong came, presumably from his own quarters under a separate roof. He found me in my bedroom and stood just beside the door.

'*Tuan* . . .'

'Where the hell's Taro? Have you had him out a walk?'

Chong didn't say anything. He didn't move. After a moment I walked over to him.

'What about my dog?'

He shook his head.

'*Tuan* . . . please . . .'

I took a deep breath.

'Go on. Tell me!'

He told me in Cantonese, a small lamenting rush of words, pitched high, as though fear put him near hysteria. I had never heard that tone coming from Chong.

Every day he had taken the dog for a walk and every day Taro had been let off the lead by the pond in the park. They went at dusk when there were no children about or women pushing prams. The last walk had been two days ago. Taro had run free in a wide arc as usual, then disappeared.

'I look. I look,' Chong said.

'You'd be near the drive?'

He nodded.

'Were there any cars on it?'

'I not know.'

'Man! You must have heard something?'

He wasn't sure about that either. Perhaps there had

been a quick, sharp yelp, but it could have been monkeys. The park monkeys have a wide repertoire of noises.

I didn't ask if he had phoned the police. You don't phone the police about dogs in Malaysia. Dogs die young in the tropics, very few of them from natural causes. Taro had seen quite a life, almost old.

'*Tuan*, for two hours I look. Then next day also.'

'You couldn't help what happened. Get me a whisky.'

I moved around the room, pulling things out of the haversack. When my drink arrived I told Chong to get me something to eat, then sat down on the bed with the glass in two hands.

I hoped Taro was dead. One swipe with a *parang*, maybe. That way it would have been quick. They hadn't left the body to be found, which meant something. I ought to be thinking about what it meant.

I wasn't a man to have a dog, away too much, leaving him with servants. I couldn't blame Chong, just myself. I might have taken Taro on the boat, but he got seasick. He didn't like cars too much, either, just his own place really, the grounds whose margins he inspected night and morning. He liked the sorties out from private territory but his real world had been those clearly marked frontiers which he defended.

Not knowing what had happened was bad. I'd wake up sometimes in the next months thinking about that. When you know you put the thing in proper perspective, an animal gone after a reasonable span. You get a replacement.

I reached out for the phone, dialling the hospital, getting through to the floor sister who told me that Russell, though making excellent progress generally, had been losing out on sleep and was rather restless. He had been given sedation early and had now dropped off. Was my call urgent? I said no, and that I'd ring again in the morning.

I had a bath, then went into the sitting-room and switched on television. Chong brought me my dinner on a tray, cold meat and a salad of limp Cameron Highlands lettuce garnished with small purple onions and sliced cucumber soaked too long in vinegar. I drank beer. Even with the noise from the set the house felt like a mortuary after the attendants had gone home. When Chong came in for the tray I tried to establish human contact.

'I don't hear much noise from the kitchen. Is it the cook's day off?'

'No, *Tuan*, he go. Grandmother sick. All family go, too. House now empty.'

I didn't ask if our cook had gone for good, all the signs were there. I wasn't too troubled, the man was Russell's choice, not mine.

'Can you manage on your own, Chong?'

'Yes, okay.'

'What about cooking?'

'I cook too.'

Dinner hadn't been much of an advertisement for his talent in this area, but his apparent faithfulness was almost touching. It couldn't have been too pleasant all alone up on this hill after Taro's disappearance, especially in a town with K. L.'s burglary rate.

The news came on the screen. In a kind of triumph over our return to a surface norm the announcer dwelt with relish on the troubles of others. A lot of places seemed to be getting it in their turn. Down in Singapore another millionaire had been kidnapped, which would see Kang on overtime. I knew the victim of the outrage slightly and didn't think his family would be in any rush to find the ransom money.

The back door slammed, Chong's signal that he had gone to his own quarters for the night. I sat watching the screen but considering petty larceny. It would be extremely interesting to see whether Russell's files had an entry on one Hsien Ho. If they did I was pretty certain that the dossier would hold a lot more information about the man than Kang had been able to give me, the personal items which from time to time Russell had chosen to read to me had all been detailed, usually running to a couple of typed pages.

I got up and went down the passage, deciding to inspect the bookcase lock before looking for instruments to use against it. I went into a room that had been tidied, cleaned, and then left. A few of the occupier's possessions were still about, giving out a feeling that they would never be used again. I turned to the bookcase which had four shelves behind glass. The upper two shelves were empty.

Still under lock and key were books on Jurisprudence, Forensic Medicine, three dictionaries, a Fowler, and a complete set of the latest Encyclopedia Britannica. The Menzies secret files had been removed. I looked in the cupboards underneath, but without hope, to find that this was where Russell kept his shoes, presumably to preserve them from damp mould.

There was no other likely place in the bedroom where those files could be, but I had a careful look anyway, this covering the windows to see if they were locked. There was also a french door on to a little verandah Russell never used, much preferring to track me down on mine. The door handle was of the turn down type, with a bolt incorporated underneath, the knob of this showing that it was driven home. I tried the handle anyway. The door opened out on to the verandah.

A neat workman had been busy. The bar of the bolt had been sawn off with a fine-bladed fretsaw just where it seemed to sink into the plate on the door frame. Whoever had done this job had taken his time over it, almost certainly breaking and entering by another route in order to have this one, meant for later use, kept as neat and tidy as possible.

I shut the door again. I could have erected some kind of defence with piled furniture, but didn't, nor did I look for the key to the door to the corridor which didn't seem to be anywhere about. Back in the sitting-room I sat down again, looking at the screen, conscious of an increased pulse rate. I switched off the set from Russell's table gadget and listened to the silence. A tiny little voice started up in my brain, not much more than a bird peeping, saying that I didn't have to stay alone in this house tonight, I could get in the Zodiac and drive down to Seremban for a late hour business conference and one of Batim's spare beds after it. I pretended I didn't hear the voice. It got louder, telling me that 'they' had killed my dog, sawn off a bolt, got rid of my cook and were paying Chong to hear nothing at all from those quarters of his across a courtyard.

Car tyres crunched over my gravel. I got up and went into the darkened hall looking through glass that flanked the front door. Someone was getting out of a car. I switched on the porch light. It was Archie Potter. He walked towards the steps like a man who is determined not to show that he's had too much to drink.

'Hello, Paul. I thought I'd chance it and see if you were back. Tried last night, too.'

'Oh?'

'Sort of personal thing. I just wanted a word with you.'

He had more of what he'd been drinking, which was whisky, then sat down without being asked, looking as though a director had shouted at him to look relaxed. He put one leg over the other and laid hold of an ankle, then grinned at me.

'Ruth told me about coming here,' he said.

I almost closed my eyes. The last thing I wanted to be concerned with tonight was the Potters' marital stress.

'We had a "Who's Afraid of Virginia Woolf?". Did you see that picture, Paul?'

'No.'

'Both our guts out all over the coffee table.'

He laughed. I didn't see the joke. I sat down.

'The thing is, she was using your suggestion.'

I couldn't remember what my suggestion had been, only that I hadn't thought much of it after Ruth had gone.

'It really worked, too. And it cut out the screaming. I suppose I was winded. Later I suddenly realized that she couldn't have hit on that cool, practical line herself. So I made her tell me. But by that time it was all right. I mean, she really understands my sexual problems now. We were able to talk about them for the first time in our marriage.'

This news would probably have cheered a psychiatrist no end, enabling him to wind up a successful case and begin thinking about his bill, but it did nothing for me.

Archie drained his glass.

'You could say we've put a big patch on our life together.'

'No Chinese girl?'

'That's right. It wasn't easy winding that up, I can
tell you. It's cost me money. You know, Paul, they're not
supposed to be all that good, but this one . . .'

He stopped and waggled the foot at the end of the leg
across his knees. If I'd given him the slightest encouragement he'd have launched forth about the girl's virtuosity
in an old craft. I didn't. Finally, after a wait, he said :

'I just wanted to thank you.'

'Sure you don't want to kick in my teeth?'

He gave me a big smile.

'Maybe I felt like that next day, but not now. Though
I still don't know why she came to you.'

'Neither do I.'

'She wasn't making a play for you?'

'I wasn't conscious of it.'

'Maybe you just didn't notice. Ruthie the femme fatale.
That's a real laugh.'

I looked at him with the feeling that if I had said
anything to Ruth that had helped tighten up the loosened
knots of her bondage to this man then probably I had
sinned. It's not true that we get the mates we deserve. It
was unthinkable that Ruth deserved Archie.

'Paul, can I have a re-fill?'

'If you think you can drive after it.'

'I can drive any time.' He stood. 'How about you?
You haven't a glass.'

'You can give me a small malt. Not much.'

If I hadn't been watching I wouldn't have seen Archie
make my drink something just slightly more than straight
malt. He was deft enough, about as efficient as a parlour
magician, and then took quite some time over preparing
what he wanted for himself. There was no problem in seeing
that I got the right glass, his was almost full, and not three-
quarters water.

'Cheers,' he said.

I put the malt down on a table by my chair. He tried
not to keep looking at it but was suddenly as jumpy as my

late dog at the threat of thunder. It was no good pretending to sip the whisky while I actually poured it down inside my shirt, the way he was staring he'd notice any drop not going where it was supposed to. Also, I've never been any good at conjuring.

Archie's smile had shifted over from his normal bright boy at the bar performance into a rictus grin. I was tempted to ask whether the tablet dissolved in my malt was lethal or just sedation. The streak of sadism in my nature . . . which I insist is only ribbon wide . . . would have enjoyed seeing this man crumple. I didn't think it would take much to make that happen, or to shake out of him the little he knew, but I was damn certain he knew very little indeed. Archie just couldn't be more than a message boy doing a job for the price of a small retainer. Personally I'd have taken care to find a better message boy but it was more than likely that the people behind him had no alternative available. And in his way he had served me. I wanted him to leave fairly happy, stopping by the nearest public phone to report mission accomplished.

'I think I'm going to chuck you out of here, Archie. I'm suddenly feeling pretty exhausted.'

'Aren't you going to drink your malt?'

He couldn't not say it.

'After I've climbed into bed. And with a couple of aspirins.'

I could practically hear the clanking of his thoughts then. Chewed up aspirins were going to mask any slight bitterness that might remain in my drink. Also, I had admitted to being tired. This was near enough for him to put in an affirmative report and collect his fee.

He stood.

'Okay, I'm off. Paul, you won't say anything to Ruth about my coming here?'

'No.'

'The thing is, I think we should play everything down now. To stop all the talk. That's what's still worrying Ruth, the gossip.'

I had no comment on that, just saw him to the door, locking this before he was down the steps, ramming home a bolt that was rarely touched and needed oiling. I was back in the sitting-room turning out lights when I heard the sound of gravel crunching again.

The malt went down my bathroom washbasin. I checked for staining on porcelain, but there wasn't any. I took the empty glass to the bedside table, placing it next to an aspirin bottle with the cap left off. Suddenly I noticed that Taro had received the only obituary a dog gets, Chong had cleared away his pad, leaving empty a long tenanted corner.

I remade the bed, simulating my body with scatter cushions arranged in a curve to suggest a sleep withdrawal into the foetal position, and the coverlet drawn high on the pillow as though I made a practice of hiding my head, too. The reading-lamp was black-shaded on an adjustable arm and I focused it down on to the empty glass and aspirin. None of this would stand up to close inspection, but it wasn't meant to, and when I went back towards the hall door for a check the whole thing seemed to have a certain artistic merit, even down to a paperback on the floor that could have fallen from a slack hand. I switched on a transistor to late evening saccharine, turning this low, then carried a chair that wouldn't let me get comfortable to just inside the bathroom.

The door opened out, which provided a screen from that other door. I pushed the chair around, testing visibility through the crack between a slab of teak and its frame, settling on a position that gave me a quarter-inch slit view in a dim light. I could just see a handle that would have to be turned down. The intruder would come from the passage, there was no other way, counting on an unlocked bedroom door in a house with a servant to bring a breakfast tray.

If the man was going to use a revolver he'd need fairly close range which ought to put him clear of my screen and let me see him in the act of raising that gun. I checked the Luger by the lamp, then went over to my sentry post.

The waiting seemed to go on forever. An hour felt like six. Drowsiness didn't threaten at all, instead tension tightened until there wasn't any slack left on the spring.

The muted radio became an irritation. I needed it as a distraction for my visitor, but it became that to me, too, and I sat there straining to get singers' words, making this a kind of idiot game. At midnight the station flashed two minutes of pre-digested news, most of which I couldn't hear, but the disc jockey who followed came over too loud and clear. He sent out over the night air a piercing, terrible jocularity in Cantonese to which he added the unspeakable practice of singing a line or two of the songs himself before giving them pick-up volume.

I didn't spot my visitor through the spyhole. He stood three feet from the bed, in black trousers and a pullover buttonless shirt. He looked dressed for skin diving through dark waters. What he carried wasn't a gun, but some kind of box, held in both hands. This was big enough to hold a mini typewriter. He held the thing pushed out in front of him, as though offering a gift package to the bed.

The shape on it seemed to be worrying him. He didn't put the box down but turned his head towards me. It was Hsien Ho. I couldn't fire the Luger from my thigh, I had to lift it. He saw the movement. His body pivoted for a throw. I fired at the box as it left his hand.

There was a boom, then a flash like a vastly magnified magnesium flare. I was blinded for seconds. More than that seemed to have happened to Hsien. He screamed. His hands came up to his face. Flames from burning shirt sleeves ran up fingers into his hair.

The flaming ball on the floor was red now, like a beating heart, expanding from a series of explosions at its core. Fire jumped on to my bed, flaring yellow and green. It ran in hideous, quicksilver eagerness over flooring. I began to feel its sucking greed for oxygen.

A human torch toppled forward. Flames flared up around it. Hsien was making no sound now.

The door handle took skin off my fingers. I fought suction to shut myself in the bathroom. As the lock clicked fire tongues probed at floor level, tasting the tiling.

It seemed to take a long time to get the window open and I caught my foot on the sill, falling into a flowerbed beneath. The roaring back in the bedroom sounded like all the jets turned on in a monster oven. While I was running around to the front of the house there was a thud followed by an explosive increase in noise. Fire burst through the main roof, shooting up sparks and sizable pieces of timber, following these with a long twisting snake of greenish-red flame. There was no wind but the trees around the garden shivered.

Half-way to the garage I looked back again just as Chong came running out of his quarters. He was making for the kitchen door. I waved to him but he didn't see me. Before I could get to him he had climbed steps and put a key in a lock.

He was spun about by that rush intake of air; his skull face painted a mottled pink. He put up his hands as Hsien had done. I dragged him clear.

'What did you think you were doing?'

I couldn't hear his answer in the roaring. I had to haul the man towards the garage. He stood by it waiting while I backed out the Zodiac and never moved as I swung the car around. He was neatly dressed, white tunic, black trousers. Then, while I shouted at him to get in the car, he turned slowly and looked back towards the house.

Fire was sweeping from room to room. Windows that had been dark suddenly glowed. The hole in the roof was an enlarging crater throwing up burning brands that came down on lawn and gravel. Tiny embers were burning holes in the Zodiac's bonnet paintwork.

'Chong! We can't do anything. Get in!'

At the foot of the drive I heard fire sirens. I turned the car right, into the quiet road through the park. From half a mile away my house on its hill looked like a beacon lit to warn a city.

I slept through breakfast in one of Batim Salong's too soft beds, joining my co-directors for morning coffee on the patio, wearing starched shirt and shorts that had been laid out for a refugee. We sat in white painted chairs with a swimming-pool to starboard, all of us as jumpy as Hollywood executives committed to a seven million dollar film they now suspect the public aren't going to take to their hearts. Akamoro, in particular, was giving out stress signals. He leaned forward, clasping his hands together.

'Mr Harris, I do not understand? You are now in hiding?'

'Temporarily.'

'But . . . for what reason?'

'I want the police to believe I'm still at sea on my boat. The press aren't going to make a feature story out of a man's house burning down while he's away. Even Chong's supposed bones won't provide much in the way of human interest. No weeping widow available, not even any relations. Chong's death is only going to rate a four-line mention on page three.'

Batim was looking at me with some distaste. I couldn't blame him. Not only had I roused practically his entire household in the small hours of the morning demanding hospitality, but I'd also insisted, to a slightly hung over host, that he despatch his chauffeur at once to Kuantan in the Zodiac. The man was to leave the car by the jetty where it had sat during my absence in Kelantan and then come back himself on the K. L. bus, not gossiping en route. I didn't think the local police, when alerted, would notice small burns on the paintwork and these ought to be masked by travel dust anyway. The *Tanjong Pudu* was already at sea, ordered to sail by phone, Busir to take her on an extended cruise to the Great Natoena Islands during which the boat was to keep strict radio silence.

'You won't get away with this,' Batim said. 'It only needs one man who saw you last night on land to blow the whole thing to pieces.'

'I don't think anyone did see me on land. Unless it was your cousin in Kuantan. You ought to be able to shut him up easily enough.'

'You rang the hospital.'

'I didn't say from where. It could have been my boat. The news about Russell was good. There was no need for me to give up my holiday and come home.'

'But there is Mr Potter!' Akamoro wailed.

I looked at the Japanese.

174

'Right at this moment Archie will be thinking he could be pinned down as an accessory to murder. And he'll be scared out of a couple of years of his natural life. I'd hate to be him this morning. He'll know that any charred bones turned up are mine, not Chong's. Chinese servants tend to disappear when there's trouble, in case they're accused. And the last time Archie saw me I was bound for bed with a knock-out potion in my hand. He never saw my car, which was in the garage with the doors shut. Nothing will make him believe that I got away. I'm betting on Archie being the last man to challenge any police theory that strikes a light note over this whole business.'

Batim stayed critical.

'You're assuming that Potter didn't know this man Hsien was coming after him?'

'You bet I'm assuming that. Archie was scarcely on the fringe, certainly not in the picture. Nobody in their senses would take that man into their confidence, particularly the crowd who were after me.'

'You sound as though you know who they are?'

'I think I know who they are but I've no proof.'

'You believe this game you're playing will get that proof?'

'I can't see any other way of getting it.'

Batim's smile wasn't pleasant.

'You appreciate of course, Paul, that in asking me to hide you here you could put me in a very awkward position?'

'The way you're situated in this life no one could put you in a very awkward position. Especially under the kind of regime we have at the moment. I'm not worried for you, Batim.'

'That was obvious.'

Akamoro was massaging his hands.

'Mr Harris, there has been an attempt to kill you. Do you think this is in any way connected with Kelantan Developments?'

'Most certainly I do.'

'In other attacks on you your life was not in danger?'

'No, it wasn't.'

'You do not now believe these attacks connected with Min Kow Lin?'

'I'm sure they weren't.'

'But why save your life when it is easy to kill you and then last night go to much trouble to arrange murder?'

I looked straight at Akamoro.

'Earlier it was too soon to have me out of the picture. Kelantan Developments hadn't been set up. Now it has been.'

'I do not understand.'

'I'm sorry to make a mystery of this, but until I have some concrete evidence I must. As yet my theory could be very far out.'

'I must ask one more question, Mr Harris. Surely these people who wish to kill you become suspicious when their man Hsien does not return to report?'

'Why? If your man does his job, and it's pretty obvious he has, what is there to report? I'd say that it was planned that after he'd used that incendiary bomb Hsien was to get clear fast. Probably right out of the country.'

'I see. So they cannot know that their plan has failed?'

'Not if I don't turn up. And if I'm still out of the picture when it is pretty obvious I should be right in it they're not going to believe that I'm enjoying sea breezes on my boat. My absence will finally confirm that they got me.'

Akamoro patted his cheeks with a handkerchief. It was warm on the patio in the sun, but not hot, a cooling breeze reaching high ground.

'The time has come to make a public announcement about Kelantan Developments,' I said. 'I hope that my co-director will agree to this?'

Batim stared. He didn't move in his chair.

'The sooner the better, really. Tomorrow morning, perhaps? Early enough for coverage in the evening papers. The press will be invited of course, and the proceedings presided over by His Excellency. You, Batim, will regret the absence of the other member of your board, on account of an unavoidable business trip. It may seem a little odd you appearing on your own like that, but it will also show who is boss.'

Akamoro twitched slightly, then was still again.

'Forgive my ignorance of these matters,' Batim said. 'But why the hell give a press conference before we've done anything?'

'To show that we're pure in heart from round one, hiding nothing from the public, with only the country's best interests in mind. If this field really is a big one it could be the most important commercial development in Malaysia in the last two decades. There will be a great deal of interest in it. Your speech is likely to prove more important than any given by a politician in the next six months.'

'Indeed? We'll work on the text together, no doubt?'

'Mr Akamoro and I will give you every possible assistance we can.'

'Thank you. I have the feeling that you are also hoping that my speech will force your enemies out into the open. Is that correct?'

'Yes,' I said.

CHAPTER XI

BATIM SALONG was in bed, playing solitaire on a board across his knees. Our dinner together had not been particularly cheerful. It wasn't that we were both missing Akamoro, now back in his Kuala Lumpur hotel, but more a kind of hangover from the Tunku's first major public appearance.

I had listened to a tape of the entire performance and I thought it had all gone off very well on the whole in spite of the fact that Batim had been somewhat startled by the probing of reporters at question time. He had expected rank to act as a shield against any impertinence from the press only to find that once you enter commerce it doesn't matter a damn if you are a prince. But as far as the speech itself was concerned His Excellency had shown a top actor's skill at putting over words which meant nothing at all under any kind of analysis but still, during the delivery, rang with integrity. He was, in fact, a natural and as a politician would have had cabinet rank in no time at all. I was pretty certain he would survive in business, too, with a little guidance here and there, and there was no doubt about the splendid presence he would make at the annual general meeting.

He lifted a card, then put it back again. I was sure he was cheating. Without looking up he said:

'Our Japanese friend has not telephoned to congratulate me.'

'Probably too busy on the line to Tokyo.'

'Do you think it is possible that he already mistrusts us?'

'Yes.'

'This doesn't disturb you?'

'It's a slightly unfortunate start for Kelantan Developments but I don't think we should let that trouble us too much. Perhaps, though, another time when you're answering press questions it would be a good idea not to strike the note of Malaysia for the Malaysians quite so hard.'

'You think that's what worried him?'

'It would worry me if I were working for Hawakami.'

'I appear to have a lot to learn. It rather reminds me of being with my tutor in Oxford. I quarrelled with my tutor.'

'Don't quarrel with me, Batim.'

'I have, as a matter of fact, a bone to pick with you. I didn't want to spoil our appetites by doing it over dinner but I really am rather angry.'

'Oh?'

'Some man of yours rang in from Kota Bharu. It was while you were having your swim.'

'That would be Bahadur.'

'He used the code word Jawa. This is not to be given to all and sundry. I insist on my privacy here being respected. There is a public number for my secretary. Jawa is for me personally.'

'I'm sorry, Batim. But I wanted him to get through to

us direct when he could confirm the purchase of that rubber estate. Is it fixed?'

'It would appear so.'

'I'll ring Akamoro.'

Batim ignored this.

'Now I'll have to change the code word, which is a nuisance. You will not do anything like this in future.'

'All right.'

He looked at me.

'The man seemed worried about you.'

'Bahadur? That's interesting.'

'I think I frightened him somewhat. Apparently he had been expecting Akamoro. Why do you use a Sikh for your assistant?'

'I had a Japanese for a while, but he got married and went home. I was looking for someone from a neutral race. A Tamil wouldn't do. Also, Bahadur is fairly tough and will get tougher.'

'You trust him?'

'To quite a degree.'

Batim laughed.

'The philosophy of Harris. Those you love you trust to quite a degree.'

'I don't love Bahadur.'

'Nonsense. He was as agitated as if you had been his father. Or, to flatter you, an elder brother. He'd been reading a K. L. paper with that item about your house. Instinct, perhaps, told him that you weren't as far from that fire as we've been pretending. I had to give him my word that there was no question of you being incinerated. He took some convincing since I couldn't say that you were splashing in a pool only yards from me. I'm not sure he believes you're on your boat, but he no longer thinks you were those bones. Also, he appreciates the need to keep his mouth shut about you still being with us.'

'Thanks for doing all that.'

'What plans have you for this youth?'

'He thinks that if he hangs on I'll make him a director.'

'And will you?'

'Maybe.'

'Well, don't bring him here. I don't like Sikhs. I can't stand their beards or their shining eyes. And they're a dissolute lot.'

I laughed. Batim moved another card, then two more in quick succession. He reached for cigarettes and lit one.

'Don't you think you could now tell me what we're waiting for?'

'I'd rather hang on to see if it happens. If it does explanations won't be necessary.'

'You're expecting a phone call? To me?'

'To the chairman of Kelantan Developments.'

'I see. You don't look too comfortable in that chair. Would you like some music?'

'No thanks.'

'We might play gin rummy?'

'I always lose.'

'Paul, I've never seen you looking like this before.'

'How do I look?'

'Jumpy and grim at the same time.'

'That's how I feel.'

'If this call comes how do I know it's the one you're expecting?'

'You just will.'

'God! Now you're making me tense. I hate mysteries.'

'I don't like making them. But I could still be wrong.'

'You hope you are?'

'Yes.'

'Go and mix a drink for yourself. There's nothing here. I don't keep it by me any more. And you'd better drink it in the other room. I don't particularly want to see you with your glass.'

It was me he didn't want to see for a while.

I went along to the drawing-room with its huge windows opening out on to the patio and the pool. I poured a whisky and sat down with it. The lamps were soft, I could see moonlight over the walled grounds though cloud was building up, perhaps for a thunderstorm. It was half-past nine, getting late. I could be wrong.

I didn't hear the phone bell ring, it wasn't the Jawa number. A servant passed along the corridor and then came back again. A moment later an ivory instrument on a desk near me gave a faint tinkle as the call was switched through to the private line. I got up, walked over to the desk and picked up the receiver.

It was Batim I heard first.

'. . . I find this completely unbelievable.'

'Your Excellency, it's the last thing I want to have to believe myself. But I have no alternative. I've been given what amounts to positive proof.'

'Indeed? What proof?'

'A witness. Who was with Paul on the night he died. Only hours before it actually happened. Paul did come back to K. L. He *was* in that house when it burned down.'

'You mean perhaps that he was in the house before it burned down?'

'I'm afraid I don't. There was no reason for him to leave it again. He was tired. He stated that he was going to bed with a sedative. In fact, Paul was practically on his way to his room when my witness left. And he'd been drinking. They both had.'

'When did you get this information, Mr Menzies?'

'Tonight. I've been in a state of shock since. I'm in hospital. I've been very ill.'

'So I was told.'

Batim's voice stayed cold. This seemed to worry Russell.

'Your Excellency, it's horrible for me to have to tell you this. Much worse to have to accept it for myself. But on thinking the matter over I felt you should know at once, in view of your connection with Paul over this new company.'

'I see. But Mr Menzies, I still don't believe that Paul is dead. Intuition, perhaps. There is a strong strain of this in my family.'

There was a pause. I stared at the whisky I hadn't finished.

'Your Excellency, have you tried to get in touch with the boat?'

'Oh, yes. There's no reply.'

'Because he isn't on board! I doubt if those Dyaks know how to operate a radio telephone.'

'Have you been in contact with the police about this?'

'No, I couldn't stand their questioning tonight. To-morrow.'

'Why doesn't your witness go to the police?'

'Well . . . he came to me first. An old friend. He's been out of town. He only just learned about the fire. He got in his car and came to the hospital.'

'Who is this man?'

'Mr Potter.'

'Ah, yes, I've heard of him. Commercial something or other.'

'Your Excellency, I must again impress on you the seriousness of all this.'

'Why impress this on *me*, Mr Menzies?'

'Well, it's a matter of Paul's affairs.'

'Indeed?'

'What has happened means that I'm now the sole surviving partner in Harris and Company.'

Batim was responsible for the silence then. It lasted for almost a minute.

'The *sole* partner, Mr Menzies?'

'Yes. We always meant to bring in someone else. We had a third partner, a Japanese, but he resigned. And that was before I came north. I've always handled most of the company's legal business even when I had my own practice in Singapore. When I retired from that I came up here. Gradually I took over more and more of the administration of Harris and Company.'

'Paul never told me about this.'

'Your Excellency, I don't like saying it, but he tended to play down my role in the business. I rarely went in to the office. It was best that I didn't.'

'I see. So Harris and Company is now your company?'

'That is roughly the legal position. It has yet to be established, of course. But I don't doubt that it will be. An exception is the diesel factory in Johore which has other directors. They may or may not elect me to their board, though I expect they will. However, the parent company here in Kuala Lumpur will pass under my control quite quickly. In my view it could be said that Kelantan Developments is something of an offshoot of the parent company. I think that would have been Paul's view. It's certainly mine.'

'You expect to be elected to our board in his place?'

'That's perhaps not an immediate matter, Your Excellency, but I felt that I must point out that Paul's interests are now my interests.'

'For a man who was recently in shock, Mr Menzies, you have made a remarkable recovery.'

'Please don't misunderstand me . . .'

'Oh, I don't think I am at all. It was good of you to get in touch. And, of course, when Paul's death has been established we will no doubt have to be in contact again.'

'I was hoping for a meeting with you shortly?'

'That may be quite difficult to arrange, Mr Menzies. Good night.'

After a moment I went down the passage to the bedroom. Batim was propped up against pillows, his arms straight down on the cover.

'You listened?' he asked.

I nodded.

'What are you going to do?'

'Visit the sick. Will you lend me a car?'

'Come back here afterwards.'

'It'll be late, Batim. I'll go to an hotel.'

'I'm sending you in the Rolls. It will bring you back.'

The receptionist didn't quite know what to do with someone wanting to see a patient at eleven-thirty pm. She was Chinese and pretty, her black hair straight and in a geometric line across her forehead, making a three-sided frame.

'I'm sorry, sir, but it's quite impossible at this time.'

'He has a private room and hasn't been sleeping too well recently. I think he'll be glad to see me. Why not ask the ward sister if it would be all right?'

'But it's against regulations!'

'They can be waived sometimes. The matron's a friend of mine. Could I speak to her?'

'She's not in the hospital.'

'I'm sure she'd authorize this. I mayn't be able to see Mr Menzies for a very long time if I don't tonight. If he's asleep we won't disturb him. But if he isn't, what harm can it do? Try the ward sister.'

'Oh . . . all right. What's your name?'

'Hsien Ho.'

She stared. I smiled.

'An old joke between Mr Menzies and me.'

The receptionist picked up the phone. It didn't seem to me she was putting my case too well to the ward sister. She hung up. There was a five-minute wait during which the girl didn't appear to notice me at all. Then the buzzer went. The receptionist seemed surprised by the message.

'Sister says it's all right. Mr Menzies wants to see you.'

'I thought he would.'

'Fourth floor. The lift's over there.'

I worked the cage myself. There was a mirror in it, presumably to remind visitors that they ought to bring smiles in with them from the outside world. I didn't think I was looking my best.

The ward sister was waiting in the corridor. She was Chinese, too. She came towards me, then stopped.

'But . . .? You're not Mr Hsien!'

She remembered a tall Manchu.

'I'm deputizing for him.'

'I'll have to check with Mr Menzies. We can't have just anyone coming in here in the middle of the night. What's your name?'

'I'm his business partner. I've been away. But I talked to Russell a few times on the phone. I expect he's been using it a lot?'

'He pays for the privilege,' she said crisply.

We were walking along together. I was ready for the first check in her movement. I put out my hand to a knob.

'Don't announce me. I won't be in here for very long.'

The sister didn't know whether to raise the alarm or not. I went in, shut the door again, and leaned back on it.

Russell's bed was against the corridor wall. He was propped up under a moveable arm lamp that shone straight down on him. He had been reading the financial section of the *Straits Times*, but had given this up. He turned his head, seeing only a shape. He lifted an arm and flipped the light beam on to me.

'I'm doing the interrogating, not you,' I said.

I went over to the bed and put the light back on to him. His skull shone pink through the sparse hairs covering it. He didn't move. There was no change in his colour at all, no suggestion that he was in shock or anything remotely like it.

I walked to the footboard where I could see him better and stood beside his progress chart. I was now right in his line of vision, but he was interested in the black square of a window to my left. They had certainly trimmed down his weight in here as well as taking pieces out of him. His complexion was still pasty, but his eyes weren't so deeply buried in age pouches.

'Hsien was cremated,' I said. 'Chong's with me now.'

The door to the corridor opened.

'Is . . . everything all right, Mr Menzies?'

He didn't look at her.

'Quite all right, Miss Tong.'

'Ten minutes then. No more.'

She shut the door slowly, trying to see me as she did it. We heard the lock click. Russell continued to look at nothing. I pulled up a chair and sat.

'A computer has been working in my head,' I said. 'It came to a machine conclusion. I didn't want to believe it. I kept re-punching the evidence cards and putting them in again. Same conclusion came out. When did you decide to become Singapore's Philby?'

He moved against the pillows as if to get more comfortable. He raised an arm and shoved up the light, bringing me into its range. Then he swept the newspaper off the coverlet.

'Nineteen forty-eight,' he said.

'When Mao was pushing Chang out of China?'

'Yes.'

'You believe that all South East Asia is going to belong to Mao?'

'I believe it will be Communist. Mao has probably been dead for years. The Russians put their myth in a glass coffin embalmed. The Chinese have kept theirs alive, as a matter of policy.'

'Wouldn't you get the chopper from your friends for saying that?'

'Not while I remained useful to them. I wouldn't give much for my chances if I ceased being that.'

'So it's not a faith with you?'

'I have no faith. I've never had one.'

'Reason tells you that this is the road to a good world?'

'Certainly not. I merely think it is inevitable that Communism will win. Capitalism as a dynamic has spent itself. It's worn out. And not only in South East Asia. The sooner it is finished off the better.'

'You speed the process with killings?'

'It doesn't take you long to get sentimental, does it? Yes, I do that when necessary. Which is not to say that I like doing it. We are up against a current in history which can't be diverted. The facts are there, to be rejected by the emotional, accepted by realists. I am a realist. That doesn't mean that I like all aspects of what is happening and what will happen.'

'You weren't just trying to secure your own position with the Reds?'

'At my age you don't bother about securing your own position. You only want to go on being useful. In our time there is only one way to have a function. Become part of the current. That's what I've done. It's what I decided to do more than twenty years ago. With my eyes open and without sentiment.'

Russell looked totally composed. We might have been having a chat on the verandah.

'What would you have done with my business?'

'Run it better than you've been doing.'

'And when you died?'

'I'd have seen that there were other directors to take over.'

'Undercover Reds?'

'That's as good a label as any other, I suppose. There's a wide selection to choose from in this country, and in some surprising places.'

'You'd have been bleeding capitalism to speed its collapse?'

'Why not? The sooner it dies of anaemia the better. Its death throes have resulted in misery to millions.'

Russell was unassailable. I tried another tack.

'How did Archie feel about those bones amongst the ashes?'

'Hysterical. Embarrassing in a hospital. I had to calm him down. Money is his sedative. He has an itch for it that transcends moral considerations. His world has made him what he is. In a different world he might have put up a better show, who can say? As it is he's a nothing. I recommend that you treat him as such.'

'Hsien wasn't a nothing. Do you regret his death?'

'The man blundered, or you wouldn't be here.'

'Did he burn down those rubber sheds on your orders? To speed up a sale?'

'I wouldn't have ordered anything so stupid. Not with Min already out of the picture. Hsien had his blind areas. Also, he was an activist. He liked arson and violence. Enjoyed using both. Did his mistake start your computer?'

'Yes.'

'What finally convinced you I wasn't a father figure?'

'You'd ordered your files to be removed from a house that was to be burned down. Where are they?'

'Where you'll never find them. They represented twenty years of work. It never occurred to me you'd go into my room on your first night home. Why did you?'

'To see what your records said about Hsien Ho.'

'Of course. Actually, he wasn't in them. Well, I blundered, too.'

'You've been pretty active for a man recovering from a major operation.'

'I came out from the anaesthetic knowing I had to be.

You can do a remarkable amount with a telephone and a few selected visitors, even while you're feeling very ill indeed. As I was, for a while.'

'You got help in here. I'd say from the ward sister. Is she an undercover Red?'

He smiled.

'Try to prove that. Miss Tong is highly esteemed in this hospital. Particularly with the dying rich.'

'You had a plant inside Min Kow Lin?'

'I wouldn't call him a plant. He's been there for years. Worked up to second executive echelon, but not in a position to siphon off any of their profits. I was as keen as you were to see that they didn't get that oil. But the doubts I expressed about you being able to fight Min alone were real enough. I didn't believe you'd be able to work through Batim Salong.'

'When I did, and set up Kelantan Developments, I as good as signed my own death warrant? Or was I down for elimination whether or not I put Harris and Company into the big money?'

Russell was looking past me again, at the black square of the window. After a moment he said :

'You've won. How does it feel?'

'Better than being dead.'

Russell stirred against those pillows.

'You'll find I've played fair, Paul. Winner take all, whichever way things went. I haven't left a penny of my money to party funds via the cover of a Chinese charity in Gemas. My will says you get it. Somewhere around two hundred thousand pounds. A useful sum. Especially now that your commercial horizons are expanding.'

'The idea was that no one could possibly suspect you of murdering your heir?'

'Partially, perhaps. But I also had a curious desire to be just in this matter. Probably something from my old-fashioned legal training. Before I came East I was apprenticed to a rigidly reputable firm in London. They would never touch a divorce case or anything with the slightest hint of a smell to it. Their kind have quite died out now. In law as in everything else it's a case of the survival of the adaptable. Don't do anything quixotic with my money like endowing the wing of an orphanage. It was all earned by the sweat of my brow in Singapore. Buy yourself more shares in corruption.'

The effect of that raised lamp was to shadow Russell's eyes. There was other lighting in the room I could have switched on, but I wasn't interrogating the man in the bed, in fact I never had been.

'You could change that will in five minutes,' I said. 'All you'd have to do is call in Miss Tong.'

'I could, but I won't.'

'What do you think I'm going to do?'

'Fry me.'

'I'm not going to the police.'

That seemed to amuse him.

'Of course you're not. Because you haven't the beginnings of anything the police or a prosecutor could make into a case. I could have everyone laughing at your accusations in ten minutes. For one thing, I could prove that you kept me right outside the Kelantan Developments scheme, that I knew nothing about it until I read the papers today.'

'When did you actually find out? Were you listening the night I brought Akamoro home?'

'I was. In the passage. It was bad for my legs, but worth it. Though I shouldn't have set a tail on you so soon. The trouble was Hsien was handy, and I decided to use him. It's always a temptation when you have a qualified man on the spot.'

'I'm waiting to hear what you think I'm going to do.'

'That's easy, offer an old man his life, like the softie you are. But on your terms. I get out of this part of the world for good. And you could certainly see that I did. Just a word to Batim Salong and another to your friend Inspector Kang down in Singapore who doesn't love me too much. Both or either could make it quite impossible for me to go on living in their areas. I'm not going to make it easy for you, Paul. I'm not going back to Britain.'

'I wasn't thinking of Britain. Your friends would look after you. You're fit to travel.'

'You want me to do another Philby, don't you? With perhaps twenty-four hours' grace? So that you can sleep better at nights? I'm sorry to disappoint you, but that isn't for me. Philby pretends to like it in Moscow, but I know I wouldn't enjoy Peking. Particularly as a loser. The Chinese have a national intolerance towards losers, it's part of their strength. But thanks for your kind offer. I must say it earns my contempt. I've lived the way I planned to live and I'm not compromising now. Nor am I accepting charity. Particularly from you.'

'How do you assess me, Russell?'

He laughed.

'That's asking for it. All right. You're a man of some potential who has ruined that potential by stubbornly refusing to look at the truth about the age we live in. There was a time when I hoped that you might be brought to see the facts.'

'And join your team?'

'I don't deny having my moments of sentimental weakness. The idea of leading you to the light appealed to the missionary in me. But I gave it up. You're an idiot romantic. That can't be changed. You'll go on having that dream of yourself on a white horse carrying a spear. For my part I've never been able to believe that St George killed his dragon. I think the beast is still alive and still breathing fire.'

The door opened. I don't think Miss Tong had been listening, or would have heard much if she had tried to. They build these upper floor cells for the rich with excellent sound-proofing. But she was looking worried. She stared at me.

'It's been more than fifteen minutes,' she said. 'Mr Menzies, you really must try to get some sleep now.'

Russell nodded.

'I agree.'

I stood and looked down at him.

'Goodbye, Russell.'

He didn't say anything.

In the lobby the receptionist was frosty.

'Mr Menzies used to live with me,' I said. 'I'm practically next of kin. I think you should have my present phone number.'

She pulled forward a pad and picked up a Biro.

'Name?'

'Paul Harris. The number is Seremban 2-9341.'

'That will be filed, Mr Harris.'

I went out through glass doors and across to the parking-lot. Batim's driver saw me coming and brought the Rolls forward. I opened a door and got into the air-conditioned rear compartment. All the metal fittings were silver plate. These included a small, bracketed vase holding a single rose that had come to Malaysia by air. It was full-blown and the draught I made caused a great dropping of petals.

I couldn't seem to get comfortable in the bed, too hot even with air conditioning. The room was a sealed vacuum of silence cushioned in the greater silence of the night beyond. If there were noises in the jungle I couldn't hear them. Batim's secretary's line to the outside world was switched through to an instrument by me. I had been expecting the bell for a long time, but when it came it was like a scream.

The matron of the hospital wasn't very far from hysteria. Her personal security and her reputation for efficiency were involved, and she was looking for someone to blame. She made an attempt to question me as to why I had visited Russell at that hour but got lost in the middle of this. She mentioned the police with horror. They were in the building. Long before I could ring off Batim had appeared in the doorway wearing a long silk dressing-gown. He waited until the receiver was back on its hooks.

'Well?'

'Russell is dead,' I said. 'He jumped from the fourth floor on to a cement court. Dived is more like it. He had to go head first with the swing-over windows they have. They're not easy to open, either. He had to climb on a chair. It's their first suicide. If you can call it that.'

Batim came across the room and stood by the bed.

'I believe in the death sentence,' he said. 'It's essential to any well-ordered society. It's false humanity to take up any other position.'

I looked up at the humanitarian.

'Paul! Are you blaming yourself? What else could you have done?'

'Found a way to show mercy.'

'Oh, God! He was an evil old man.'

'What we could all become in our time. Without too much extra effort.'

'You'll have perspective in the morning. I hope. Got a sleeping tablet?'

'I don't want one.'

'I'll tell them to bring breakfast in here about half-past ten. We can talk then?'

He went out. I didn't think I would want to talk about Russell Menzies at half-past ten. Or ever.

A cock crowed though it was still dark. It seemed strange that they kept hens at this palace. Then I remembered that Batim bred fighting cocks, birds fitted with special steel spurs for combat, trained to kill or be killed.